THE UGLY PRINCESS

The Legend of the Winnowwood

THE UGLY PRINCESS

PRINCESS

The Legend of the Winnowwood

Henderson Smith

Dedication

For all the girls who stand on the sidelines wishing they too could be beautiful. I hope you will let Olive show you how beautiful you truly are and the power that you already wield. Open your eyes to your own magic!

Contents

Preface

What would you give up to be beautiful? I don't mean attractive, or pretty or any other term you could conjure up to describe that thing most women seek to be or most men seek to be with. I mean staggeringly beautiful, men falling at your feet with hopeless adoration as they gaze upon you dumbfounded. *That* beautiful. I could become that beautiful if I chose, but only with a steep price. Would you pay the price? Does that call to *your* heart?

It doesn't call to mine. Yes, when I look at the girl in the mirror, I see a young woman of average height and slight build. I see her lovely emerald green eyes and I see her coarse, orange hair poking out in all directions like some unnatural haystack. I see the forty-seven warts that line her face, which accompany one large lump and two small boils. You'd probably think that I would be more than eager to trade for the great gift of beauty because I know some, if not all of you, would call me hideous. But I don't think of myself as ugly.

I think of myself as powerful, strong and fierce — for I have magical powers — powers that amaze and terrify me at times. And today is the most important day of my life, because today my mother will say the words over me and seal my fate. For I, Olive, am the last of the Winnowwood and this is my story.

1

The Legend Of The Winnowwood

Four hundred years ago, there were over five hundred of us, sisters who shared powers we were born into. Powers that gave us dominion over nature. I only know a few stories that have been passed down mother to daughter over the generations, but the clearest remembered is the killing story – the curse that was put on our kind by an evil witch named Cassandra Dragon Slayer.

It was during the time of dragons and dark magic that the Winnowwood came out of the shadows and into the history of humans, much to our own ruin. My mother said it was because our hearts were too tender, that we could not continue to turn a blind eye to the witches and how they terrorized the poor humans. The witches hunted the human children down, then ate their still-beating hearts to prolong their own evil lives. That would be the most wretched, horrific act I could imagine and I'm not sure if it's true, but I like to think it is — that it was something that heinous that forced my ancestors into action thereby sealing our own doom.

The Winnowwood knew it would be easy to kill the witches, for they underestimated our powers. We, unfortunately, underestimated their wrath.

At that time, there were seventeen witches who lived in our lands. They had ignored the Winnowwood thinking us akin to odd hermits who lived in the forest with the animals for we were a shy people who hid from them as well as the humans. We had reason to hide from the humans.

Years past, two young Winnowwood had crossed the paths of two human men and barely escaped with their lives. The men thought they were trolls and tried to kill them for a reward. Trolls aren't the only creature with an unfortunate countenance, my people are ugly as well. So, the warning was passed down, "Don't speak to humans, they'll kill you for the troll reward!" For as you certainly know, humans despise ugly people and love beauty, and it is that love of beauty that would lead to the downfall of my people.

"Anhelo Eximo Fulgar Winnowwood!" That's the phrase that destroyed the witches. It basically translates into: *I desire to release lightning*! Witches hate lightning. It smites them into nothingness in less than a second, leaving a small pile of ash that could fit on the palm of your hand. Witch ash contains powerful magic, but there is no longer anyone alive who remembers how to make it work. Once there was a book that contained all of the spells, history and lore of the Winnowwood, but it has not been seen in well over a hundred years. That is really unfortunate for me, as I have so many questions, but I digress.

The story is that an elderly Winnowwood named Ursula was in the forest when she came upon a witch who was about to rip the heart out of a six-year-old, blond, human girl with green eyes. Ursula said it was the green eyes that did it — the girl had Winnowwood eyes.

Ursula warned the witch to stop, but the witch only laughed at her, her black tongue licking her lips as her dirty claws ripped the girl's dress away. The little girl managed to slip out of her dress and run towards Ursula and that was that. Ursula uttered the words and a huge bolt of lightning crackled in the sky and smote the witch.

But as fate would have it this was no ordinary little girl; she was the only child of the widower King of Alganoun. When she returned to her home, she told her father all that had happened. He sent hundreds of men into the forest to hunt for Ursula until they finally found her. The King begged her to help him kill the witches and promised he would give her whatever she wanted for the deed.

She agreed. Shortly thereafter, a great battle took place between the witches and the Winnowwood. The witches did manage to kill twelve of the Winnowwood, but no matter, the lightning was too fast, too powerful for them to fight, until there was only one witch remaining: Cassandra Dragon Slayer. In her great despair, she crafted her revenge.

It is said that at midnight on the shores of an enchanted lake, Cassandra created the knife from an evil brew filled with magic. This legend has actually been passed down via a Bear, who supposedly watched Cassandra create the blade. With this little knife (which I have seen), the Winnowwood would be tempted with their most secret desire: beauty. All Winnowwood are women, all have emerald green eyes and we all have an extra segment on our left little finger that stems out of the top joint of the finger making it look like a branch. We call that little segment the crux for it is the heart of our power. With this Blade of the Winnowwood (which has become its name, though I think Cassandra's Cursed Blade for Oblivion would be a far better one), if you cut off the crux with the blade under the light of the moon, you changed.

It did not matter if you were old (there were many Winnowwood well over three hundred years old), you regained your youth and obtained what no Winnowwood had ever had: beauty. Initially, no one understood all of the effects, so I could almost forgive them for using it, but once it was understood that you lost your magical powers if you chose to be transformed by the blade, how could one choose it? Ask my mother and sister for your answer.

Ursula was the first Winnowwood who used the blade. It was presented to her by the King who was tricked into thinking it would be a gift for the Winnowwood by Cassandra. She had disguised herself as a shaman and convinced the King that it would be the perfect reward for all the Winnowwood had done to help him.

There are few details about how all of this actually transpired, but the end of the story was always repeated throughout the ages: when Ursula cut off her crux under the light of the moon, she became the most beautiful woman any human had ever seen. The King immediately fell to his knees and begged Ursula to marry him, which she did thereby becoming the Stepmother to the little girl she had saved.

Do I need to explain the rest? Within the first year, over four hundred Winnowwood converted, filling the land with the most beautiful women the world had ever known. I think the remaining hundred only waited because every King, Prince, Earl, Count, Baron, Lord or Knight in all of the land was taken and the remaining men were basically goat herders or farmers. Not the bargain they wanted to strike I suppose, but nonetheless, slowly our numbers dwindled.

Additional little secrets of Cassandra's revenge became clear as the years passed: if you converted before you were eighteen-years-old, none of your daughters would be born as a Winnowwood. If you used any other blade to cut the finger off, you lost your powers and were stuck in your ugly body forever. Most importantly, there was no changing your mind once cut.

And the powers they gave up — I will never give them up! I am the last high priestess to the Bestiallas, which is made up of all the animals of the world. They are mine to command and to love. I can change into any animal on this earth, though I most love to change into an eagle and fly and fly and fly. I can talk to animals and they can talk to me. And I can heal the animals if they've been injured, which has come in handy on quite a few occasions as testified by the marks on my face.

In the past, the Winnowwood not only could create lightning bolts, but had true dominion over nature. They could make it rain, clear storms and many more dramatic acts, but I haven't mastered any of that, nor do I really understand how to do it. Nor, unfortunately, does my mother.

My grandmother died shortly after my mother's birth and with her death, the detailed history of the Winnowwood died with her. She knew how to create lightning bolts! The stories of my grandmother's extraordinary powers are absolutely intoxicating to me, but it was all lost. My mother floundered with understanding her powers as I flounder with mine.

So, why would anyone willingly give up these powers? Well, there is one small problem. Being a Winnowwood, we are born very plain to begin with and then every time you use your powers to change something outside of yourself, you get uglier — a wart, a small lump, sometimes a boil. It's not pretty to be sure.

Ursula had hidden her face inside a hooded cloak as her face was covered in such hideous warts, bumps and boils that it gave her the appearance of a leper. She was well over three hundred years old and was known to have healed hundreds of animals in the forest, which obviously left damage to her face and certainly the lightning bolt would have left its mark as well.

The Blade exploited that ugliness for the uglier you were the more beautiful you became when you converted, or winnowed, as the term morphed into. Ursula was very old and very, very ugly and so when she winnowed, she became simply the most beautiful woman in the world. To become so beautiful that every man who gazed upon you would fall to his knees in awe is indeed a powerful inducement, though a pathetic one in my eyes.

My mother professes that the legend of the blade states that if a Winnowwood could be loved warts and all, that she would become beautiful and retain her powers, but I don't believe her — just another jab from the grave from that horrible old witch in my opinion. But she did have her vengeance because all of the magical Winnowwood are now gone, save one — me.

2

War

⁓

One of the most important memories I have from my child-hood was the day my father declared war on me, though because of my actions, I saved our kingdom. In truth, I saved the Kingdom of Alganoun as well. In the end, none of that mattered to Father. I embarrassed him in front of all of the courtiers of the land and in his book, that betrayal is all that counted.

Roseline and I were in our room that fateful day. She played with her dolls, as I watched the parade of soldiers that arrived at our castle all afternoon. They were magnificent in their armor, their colorful banners waving in the wind, their horses in fine saddles and armored as well. I sat on the windowsill and watched it all for hours, fascinated by all of the pageantry.

From my window, I could see the hundreds of tents that now dotted the countryside: the blue tents were for the King of Alganoun's men, the yellow tents were for my father's soldiers who he had deployed as well to show his strength. There were red tents from a faraway land I was unfamiliar with, but I think their kingdom was over the mountains in the south. It made for a patchwork of color upon the land that I found captivating.

I was not sure of all that was going on (I was only eleven), or why all the men were there, but Mother had told us that her father, the Duke of High Tower, had somehow talked the men into coming to prevent a war. She wouldn't say much about this impending war only that Grandfather was very good at convincing people to be better than they were and we should not worry.

I loved my mother's father. I called him Greatpapa and he called me his little love and hugged me every time he saw me. That was very unlike my father, or his father who was obviously the King of Rosemount then. He had told me to call him King Harold and I was always to curtsy before him and he never hugged me (I guess the apple didn't fall far from the tree when I think back on that.)

"Mummy told you to stay away from the window!" Roseline huffed at me again, "We are not to be seen!" She stared up at me with her big green eyes set wide in her plain face speckled with a company of seven small warts on her left cheek.

Roseline had received all of her warts in one day when she had first learned to heal animals, and came upon a nest of robins that had fallen out of a high tree – the seven babies all broken, peeping in pain. When she returned to the castle and saw herself in the mirror with the seven little green warts, she refused to ever use her magic again and cried whenever she thought of it. Now, whenever she was fearful or worried, her hand would go to her face and over the warts.

I had twenty-one warts on my face and one small lump on my brow. I got that when I healed a bear cub whose foot had been caught in a trap – my biggest magic to date, and one I was quite proud of. It's not that I wanted the warts, but it seemed like a small price to pay to heal my friends when they needed my help.

I glared at Roseline, "They'd have to have eyes like an eagle to see me up here," but I moved back a bit.

Outside the window, a seagull winged its way west towards the setting sun headed towards the sea. I waved and it flew closer, "Hello, Seagull!" I eagerly cried out.

The seagull gave me a nod, "Hel-loooo, Princess!" dipped its wing like a wave, then swooped higher into the air as I laughed with delight.

I loved talking to animals, but Father had banned all animals from the castle. I'm sure he thought they would be spies for us and tell us everything he did or said. I guess they probably would.

I turned around and there was my mother, Princess Opal, staring at me with her hands on her hips. "Olive, I told you to stay away from the windows." She tried her best to glare at me, but I could see the slight smile on her lips.

Roseline chided me as well, "I told her, Mummy. No one wants to see an ugly, little girl!"

Mother frowned, took me gently by my arm then hugged me. "My girls are not ugly! My girls are magic!" She smiled at me and I knew all was right with the world again.

Roseline still had a frown on her face, "But Mummy, I hear them. They whisper it behind my back, but I hear them all the time!"

"Come." My mother motioned to Roseline until she joined me in her arms. "You mustn't listen to them. Ever. People don't understand our kind and when people don't understand someone else, they can be very cruel. But *we* know who we are, and we are strong, aren't we?"

"Yes, Mama," I said with as much starch in my voice as I could muster.

Roseline choked back the beginning of tears. "I don't like it. Papa says —"

"Don't listen to your father," Mother interrupted Roseline as she gently stroked her cheek, "He's simply jealous of your magic and would steal it away if he could." She laughed and began to tickle my sister, which she loved, but pretended to hate. She ran as Mother chased her about the room.

"Excuse me, mam." The droll voice of Mother's hand-maiden, Eunice, interrupted our fun. "I'm afraid it's time to dress for dinner." She quickly exited.

Mother knelt down and hugged us both in her arms, "Now remember," she whispered to us in a conspiring tone, "You are my most beautiful, courageous girls and never, ever think otherwise."

Later that evening after Roseline and I had been put to bed, I crept back out to the window. My nightgown was warm and I tucked it over my knees and hugged them close as I sat on the windowsill. The music from the banquet hall drifted out upon the evening air and I could occasionally hear a laugh or a shout. I tapped my toes to the music until it abruptly stopped.

Then I heard a shout, "This would bring peace." Another louder voice that sounded alarmingly like my father's responded, "An unjust peace!" Then more voices, "Never will I accept this!" "Better to die in battle!"

I felt badly for my Greatpapa as it did not sound as if things were going well, they all sounded so very angry. I guess this is how wars begin — with angry voices screaming at each other.

Just then, an object hurtled towards me out of the darkness. I dodged out of the way just in time as it sailed past. It was Seagull. He collapsed exhausted on the floor, "Prin.... Princess. Prin..."

"Oh, Seagull, you've come back to chat with me. How very nice of you!" I ran over and sat down next to him and petted his head. "And flying at night. I've never seen you do that."

"Prin...cess," he gasped.

"Take your time. You sound so winded. You must have flown here very fast and far indeed," I said.

"Princess. I saw...."

"You saw? You saw me sitting in the window?" There was an apprehension in me that I knew I was trying to deny.

Seagull shook his head from side to side as he continued to gasp for air. Roseline got out of her bed and sat down beside me, a fearful look on her face. "Seagulls don't fly at night." Her hand moved to her warts.

"Well, obviously they do, for he is here." I tried to ignore Roseline's concern as I turned back to Seagull, "Are you well, Seagull?"

"The sea. I saw them." He finally gasped.

"You saw who?" I asked nervously.

"Men with...with the white hair," he finally wheezed.

I bolted upright as fear began to fill me. Next to me, Roseline began to shake, "M-men with white hair?" she stammered.

The Seagull nodded. I could barely find my voice as I asked, "Spiked white hair?" The Seagull nodded again. "You saw a man with spiked white hair?" I knew I had to be sure.

The Seagull finally replied, "No." I breathed an instant sigh of relief until he uttered his next words. "I saw thousands of them."

"Eeeeeke!" Roseline cried out as she crawled faster than a lizard across the floor and under her bed.

Those were the words that bespoke our doom. The words every person in our land lived in fear of: the people with the white spiked hair were coming – the Druzazzi – treacherous butchers who would kill us all given the chance. They had almost accomplished it a hundred years ago, but my ancestors had just been able to drive them back into the sea. We lived in fear of them trying again. And now, they were coming. Tonight might be our end.

I knew I had to be brave, fearless really, but as I stared at the massive doors to the Grand Hall, my knees knocked together. I peeked into the hall and saw the angry throng of men arguing over the future of our country. I knew what I would say would change everything – there might not be a future for our country. I looked for my mother, but there were no ladies in the room.

King Harold shouted at a short man with a crown on his head. "Again, you attempt to broker a deal that will be only to your benefit!"

The King of Alganoun was a short, plump man, but his face had a look of kindness on it, or at least for my benefit, I hoped it was. He spoke his response calmly, "You speak to me so, yet it was you who broke the treaty in the first place."

"Only because I could not allow you to take advantage of my people!" King Harold bellowed.

My Greatpapa stood next to King Harold, Father was slightly to the side of them. At this moment, I was more afraid of him than the Druzazzi. I gathered all my courage, took a deep breath and ran as fast as I could the length of the hall to my Greatpapa.

All discussion stopped when I hurled myself around him. I knew what they were thinking, not only had a child dared interrupt them, but what an ugly child! I caught a glimpse of my father's face and it was red as a beet with his shame.

Greatpapa didn't seem to mind, he smiled down at me. "Child, what in the world are you doing here?"

I motioned for him to bend down and I whispered to him all that the Seagull had told me, "Thousands of Druzazzi are approaching the coastline in their big ships directly to the west of us. They are only twenty miles from shore."

He looked me in my eyes, his face filled with concern, "Are you certain, Olive?"

"Seagull would never lie to me. I know it's true." I spoke with as much conviction as I could find.

"Good girl, my little love. Now, best to go back to your room." He gave me a quick hug before he stood.

I feared for my life when I saw my father's face from the corner of my eye — it was now purple with rage as he glowered at me. It filled me with terror. I turned and ran back out of the room knowing the punishment I would certainly face in the near future. At least I'd tried to give us a chance for a future.

Through my tears, I saw the faces and heard the murmurs from the crowd as I ran, "Ugly little Princess." I ran until I reached the entry hall where I could still hear and see inside the Grand Hall. I hid in a small room across from the doors and peaked out.

The crowd was still murmuring. There were a few snickers and smug looks towards my father. I couldn't see his face from here, but I could surely imagine it. My knees started knocking together again.

Greatpapa lifted his arms for silence. In a loud voice filled with authority, he began to speak, "It is an omen of good fortune that this meeting has brought you to this place on this night."

The King of Alganoun looked at him confused, "And why would that matter?"

Greatpapa didn't say anything for a second or two, just looked at the two Kings, and then he turned to the crowd. Finally, he spoke, "I have just been informed that a large flotilla of Druzazzi is a scant twenty miles offshore directly to the west of us." He paused a moment, then his voice boomed, "THEY ARE COMING FOR US, BROTHERS!"

There was utter silence for two seconds before pandemonium broke out. So many voices shouted at once, the sound of fear filled the room, "Murderers!" "Over a hundred years since they've tried!" "They'll kill us all!" "Cannibals!" "Rapists!"

As I peeked out from the closet, I could see their faces. To the last man, they were petrified.

"SILENCE!" my Greatpapa called out. After a few moments, the clamor died down. "They must be planning on using Buckmeade pass if they are landing to our west," Greatpapa calmly stated.

The King of Alganoun stroked his short beard, "We may have enough time to set up an ambush." He looked to King Harold, "That is, if we agree to work together."

King Harold stepped forward with his hand outstretched, "Agreed."

∾

From my bedroom window, Mother, Roseline and I had watched them all ride quickly off into the night. We were filled with dread and worry for all of them, praying they could win, fearing that they wouldn't.

My mother took our hands into hers, "If things do not go well, you must promise to change into birds and fly to the glen and hide there."

"But Mummy, I don't like the forest. I want to stay with you!" Roseline wrapped herself tightly into Mother's arms.

"My darling girl, I want you to stay as well. But if we do not win this battle, we know what will happen." Though she held Roseline in her arms, she looked me directly in the eye. "These people are the cruelest of predators, there will be no mercy for any of us."

"Then come with us, Mama." I begged her, "I can protect you in the forest as well as all of my friends. They will watch over us."

She looked out the window towards the horizon as if she were trying to see the battle that was now only a few miles away and would determine all of our futures. Mother sighed in sadness, "If only we knew. We may not have much time to escape."

I quickly stood, "Let me go now. I'll find out."

"No, Olive!" she replied fearfully, "I couldn't bear for you to see it. The battle will be fierce, arrows flying, so much blood and death..."

"I promise I will stay far above it."

"Swear you will not land. You will not change into any other animal to help, no matter what you see," she pleaded with me.

I thought of what she asked. Even if my father despised me, he was still my father. If he were in danger, I knew I would want to help. And Greatpapa...I knew I would do anything to save him. So, at that moment, I changed who I was and I became a liar. I looked my mother directly in the eye, "I promise, Mama."

With that, I stood up, put my hands above my head and cried out, "Anhelo Eximo Aquila Winnowwood!" and instantly, I became an orange-colored eagle.

My mother reached down and picked me up in her hands, "Be careful my darling brave, Olive," then threw me out the window.

❧

There was a full moon out that made flying easy. I headed due west and was looking for the pass through the mountains when I heard it: the crashing of shields, the screams of the dying, and the furious tumult of battle. I circled high overhead, but could clearly see the battle raging below.

It appeared that the ambush was working for at one end of the mile-long pass were the King of Alganoun's men, wearing their blue colors, desperately fighting the most fearsome men I had ever seen.

Each man's hair was white, shaped into spikes that stuck straight up into the air. Their faces were painted the red of the color of blood; for all I knew, it probably was blood. They wore breastplates of iron and swung humongous swords that rang out with fearsome power as they hit the soldiers' shields. The Druzazzi warriors did not carry shields, so assured of their ability to overpower their enemy with their sheer force. Most fought with formidable blades in each hand. That arrogant decision would cost them dearly.

Because the pass was narrow, it prevented the Druzazzi the opportunity to overwhelm the opposing force with their sheer numbers. As I watched, a company of men, marked with the blue of Alganoun on their shields, managed to climb the cliffs and appeared on the top of the pass looking down into the canyon and launched their arrows into the Druzazzi. It was like watching a hive that got kicked and the bees swarmed out in a fury, but the bees were the Druzazzi. They tried to find shelter from the arrows, but there was none. How they yearned for those shields now! The arrows flew through the sky and the Druzazzi fell by the hundreds.

I flew onward to the far end of the pass and saw that my Grandfather's men had closed it off from escape as well. Our men fought furiously pushing the Druzazzi back farther into the pass. Soldiers with the yellow shield of Rosemount were on the top of the cliffs here as well. More arrows rained down upon the Druzazzi and they died in such great numbers that their dead bodies began to form great piles of death.

As I watched it all, high over the fray, I felt relief as it looked like the battle was well in hand. That is, until I looked to the west to the sea. Far in the distance, I saw something.

I flew as fast as I was able, covering the few miles in seconds until I could see it clearly: over a thousand Druzazzi were leaving the beach, heading directly for the pass three miles in the distance and they were moving fast. If they got there in time, they would cut off my grandfather's men from behind.

I flew back to the battle as quickly as I was able. I knew only Greatpapa would believe me, so I looked for him, but it was hard in the midst of this mayhem. Lower and lower I glided, until I was a scant fifty-feet above the ground.

In the time that I had been away, my father's men had been pushed back to the end of the pass. If they allowed the Druzazzi to breach the pass, it would be a blood bath.

On the edge of the battle, I saw one Druzazzi warrior slip through the pass and slip out the entrance past the other men locked in battle. I wondered if he was a coward, worried about saving his own life and deserting his allies, but I lost sight of him in the forest.

Flying back over the pass, I looked again for my father, but couldn't locate him amid the hellish scene below me. I wanted to cry, seeing so many men dying before my eyes, but I had to be strong. I knew that everything depended on one premise — that I would do my duty.

Finally, I spied the command tent displaying the yellow colors of my grandfather a half mile in the distance and flew as fast as my wings could carry me. I alighted quietly in a small grove of trees, and then changed back into myself. As I crept up to look into the tent, I noticed a movement in the dark behind the guard at the tent entrance. I heard a quiet gasp, and then the body of the guard slumped to the ground.

In the moonlight, I saw him — the Druzazzi warrior who had made it through the pass. He threw open the entrance to the tent revealing Grandfather and Greatpapa standing over a map, their shocked faces registered their fear.

Without a moment to think, I cried out the words, "Anhelo Eximo Lupus Winnowwood!" and jumped the Druzazzi from the back just as his sword swung towards Greatpapa. I don't know what happened, perhaps it was just the spirit of the animal taking over mine, but my teeth clenched down hard and I heard a loud snap. The Druzazzi fell to the side dead.

I tasted the blood in my mouth and the animal part of me savored it, the human part of me felt like retching. I looked at my Greatpapa with my green wolf eyes and saw that though he had fallen, he was unhurt.

Just then, a soldier charged through the entrance. His face contorted with rage as his spear rose directly at me.

"STOP!" Greatpapa screamed at the guard, as I dodged the tip that came hurtling at me.

"But sire, the wolf," he said with alarm, "I've never seen an orange-colored wolf like it."

WAR

Greatpapa got to his knees, "I know this wolf. Stand guard outside and ensure that no one enters." he firmly directed. With a last wary look at me, the guard slowly backed out of the tent. I moved closer to Greatpapa and placed a large paw upon his leg.

King Harold had stood in the back corner of the tent as all of this had transpired and only now spoke, "Are you mad? Kill the wolf!" He pulled his sword.

Greatpapa, still on his knees, looked up at the King, "Do you really want to kill our granddaughter?" then turned to me, "Olive, what has brought you here?"

I stood up on my hind legs, my paws over my head, "Winnowwood Lupus Eximo Anhelo!" and turned back into my human form. I fell into Greatpapa's arms, "Mother wanted me to see how the battle was going, but I promised not to land."

Greatpapa smiled at me, "We'll keep your secret safe."

"But there's more. More of them coming!" I frantically explained. They both asked me questions, so I described everything I had seen. Then Greatpapa made me promise to return immediately to the castle. And once again, I promised.

But tonight had changed everything I thought about myself. I was now a liar and a killer and I wasn't going back to the castle. Not until I knew the outcome.

As I flew above, I watched a large contingent of soldiers as they ran desperately through the woods setting up a second ambush. I watched as the Druzazzi fell by the hundreds. Then, as dawn broke over the land, I could finally see victory was at hand, so I flew home. There, I would face my most dangerous opponent.

～

His face was six-inches from mine as he hissed at me, "You should never have entered that hall!"

"But I didn't know where Mother was." I tried to sound like an adult, but my voice kept creeping higher and higher in tone until I was sure I sounded just like a mouse who had encountered a cat.

"YOU SHOULD NOT HAVE ENTERED! YOU HAVE HUMILIATED ME IN FRONT OF EVERYONE!" he roared again.

I wanted to say that he should be so grateful for my powers. That he should be thanking me for saving his father from that Druzazzi, for saving all of them for that matter, but I couldn't find my voice. All I could squeak out was, "Sorry, Father."

The vein in his temple pulsed with anger, "You *will* obey me, girl!"

"That is quite enough, Michael." Mother marched into the room directly to me and took me protectively in her arms. "She's an eleven-year-old little girl." She glared at Father, "She did what she thought was best."

He looked at my mother, furious, "You promised me they would not be seen at court."

My mother's voice was firm, "Be glad she was or we would not be sitting here now."

"Don't let this happen again or there will be consequences." He turned his glare back to me, his vein throbbing wildly like it would explode momentarily, "I'll take that knife and cut it off myself!" With that, he stormed out of the room slamming the door with all of his might. I was surprised when it didn't shatter into pieces from the force inflicted on it.

"Mama, you won't let him, will you?" I extended my hand and looked down at my crux.

My mother clasped my hand in hers, "No, my darling. It will always be your decision. No one else's. That is my promise to you and your sister."

Roseline, who had been hiding under her bed, finally peeked out. Her left hand extended, tears in her eyes, "Mummy, he can cut mine off. I don't like it." She crawled out, ran over and climbed into our mother's lap with me.

"You don't understand what you're saying, Roseline." My mother's gentle voice explained, "It is magic and you have no idea what power you wield."

"I don't like it, Mummy," Roseline continued to whine as she clutched one hand over her seven little warts.

I looked up at my mother's beautiful face, "I won't ever cut it off, Mama. Not ever."

She looked at me and smiled, then tenderly touched my face, "That's why you're my extra brave girl."

3

Sixteen

In the years that followed, much to my mother's disappointment, Roseline did not use her powers. In fact, she rarely left the castle at all. Instead, she focused her attention on learning all of the skills of a Princess that would help her find her Prince: studying the lineage of the gentry, dressing handsomely, dancing gracefully and attempting clever conversation (which I believe she struggled with the most). I thought her a fool and told her so often, but she'd only smile at me and say, "You're the fool, Sister, and one day you'll see that I am right."

She also found out all she could about the winnowing process. She had learned from Mother that if you looked into the ruby red blade of the knife, it reflected what you had looked like before you winnowed. It also reflected what you would look like if you winnowed.

That was no surprise to me. I already knew what I would look like if I changed. Years ago, I had realized that if I looked into water, it reflected me as the animals saw me and the animals saw me as the blade did. I grew prettier with every wart that I added to my face.

When Roseline looked into the blade with Mother, she was shocked at how ugly Mother had been before she winnowed and disappointed in what she would look like if she winnowed. Her reflection was of certainly an attractive girl, but not one who would be called stunning.

I laughed when I saw my reflection in the blade as I was much prettier than Roseline. That drove her mad, but she finally understood how the magic worked.

The earliest day my mother would agree to allow Roseline to winnow was on her sixteenth birthday, so that was the day Roseline selected. I wasn't surprised, I knew how desperately she wanted to be admired, but even I wasn't prepared for what she did that day.

Roseline had told my mother and me that she wanted to spend the day alone in the forest and that she would appear at the ceremony at the appointed time. She also had asked Father to hold a ball for her after the ceremony and invite all of the young courtiers of the land to attend, which he agreed to only after my mother assured him that Roseline would not be an eyesore. She even invited me, though I think she did it only to torment me in her way.

As much as I thought Roseline a fool, I too was looking forward to the ceremony — I wanted to see how the magic worked. If Roseline were silly enough to give her powers away, at least it would be interesting to see the magic. I couldn't help but think how disappointed Roseline would be, as we had seen how she would look and it was far short of that thing she so desired: beauty. I hate to admit it, but it made me happy.

It was a beautiful summer night, the moon high in the night sky as we gathered. It was just the family: Mother, Father, Greatpapa, Roseline and me. Father was now King of Rosemount as King Harold had died the previous year after he developed consumption and coughed himself to death. Mama said it was because he had been too foolish to come in from the rain as he was on the trail of a magnificent buck and refused to disengage. The buck still lives, and Grandfather is dead.

My mother, now Queen, wore the white silk robe of the high priestess of the Winnowwood. It was embroidered with elaborate silver stitchery that glowed in the moonlight. The Blade of the Winnowwood rested on an ornate jeweled tray. I looked at it and a shudder went down my spine as if someone had walked across my grave.

I hadn't seen Roseline all day, but knew she had returned at sunset. When she appeared for her ceremony, she was wearing a fine new gown of pink silk with intricate golden embroidery of the bodice. I was surprised to see that she also wore a thick veil attached to her crown. In her hand, she held a silver-plated mirror. She walked slowly across the courtyard to us, stopping next to Mother, "I'm ready." She placed the mirror on the table before she held out her hand.

"You must remove your veil." My mother informed her, "Your face must be fully illuminated by moonlight."

"Must I?" she asked with a note of anxiousness.

"If you want the magic to work, yes." replied Mother.

I could hear the long sigh from her, "Please, Father, Grandfather, turn your heads away."

Mother smiled, "Sweetheart, I'm sure that's not necessary."

"Turn away. I beg you!" her desperate voice pleaded.

They turned their backs to her. Only then did she remove the veil – her face was transformed! Over fifty warts now covered Roseline's face, even a boil and one small lump.

I gasped, "What have you done?"

"It doesn't matter," she hissed at me.

"Roseline, how did this happen?" my mother asked.

"Just do it! Do it now! Release me from this infernal curse!" she screamed.

Mother looked at her a moment, then turned and took the blade in her hand. "Do you desire to trade your powers forever? Is that what is in your heart?"

"With all my heart, I do." Roseline forcefully replied.

With that, Mother took the knife and sliced off the crux of Roseline's little finger.

It must not have hurt, as she made no gasp of pain. Instead, it dissolved into silvery white dust that disappeared into the soft evening breeze. A greenish glow, starting from her left little finger, quickly moved up her hand, to her arm, her shoulders, to her face, until her entire body glowed in this greenish light — brighter and brighter until you no longer could make out her features because of the brilliance of the light. Slowly, it began to dim and as her features became more distinguishable, I gasped in awe — she was utterly beautiful!

Roseline grabbed her mirror and gazed into it, momentarily transfixed by her image, her hand began to shake, "Father."

Slowly, my father turned around. I will never forget the look on his face when he saw her, it was absolute rapture. He smiled upon her with a look of utter joy, "Daughter." He held his arms open and Roseline fell into them, a look of bliss on her face.

My face must have shown my pain for my mother wrapped me in her arms, "My darling girl, don't let this change who *you* are." She held me close.

I blinked my eyes quickly, trying to keep back the tears, "I won't. I won't change. I promise."

That night passed before my eyes like some horrible dream, how my sister tormented me! And how well she had prepared, I had to give her that. Father partnered her in the first dance, the two alone in front of the crowd. She was so graceful, never missing a step, as Father led her, moving across the ballroom floor together, Father grinning like I'd never seen him before.

I looked at the faces in the crowd: the men enchanted as they gazed upon her, the women stunned by her beauty. I didn't want to stay. There was something in me brewing that I could feel and I didn't like it – jealousy. I thought I wouldn't be tempted, that I was stronger than this, but I could feel it creeping into me like a cold, unwanted spirit. Every time Father looked at her, every smile that filled his face, struck me like a blow.

I had lived my life pitying my foolish little sister, thinking her an idiot for her choices and what she wanted in her life, but now, I could see her power. Everything would instantly change and how I dreaded that. If I thought my father disliked me before, my anticipation of how I would be treated in the future made me nauseous at the thought of it.

The music ended. I watched as Roseline's eyes searched the crowd, landing upon me. "Sister. Mother. Please join us." I turned to leave the room, and then heard my father's voice.

"Olive," he stated like a command.

I turned. He motioned for me to join them. So, he saw his opportunity as well – make Olive's life a misery and she too would change. I could see the slight smirk on his lips, it was all I needed to restore some backbone. I lifted my head and walked as regally as I could towards them, careful, as I looked through my veil. I moved directly in front of him and curtsied deeply, "Father. As you command."

My mother stood next to my father, her eyes filled with concern for me. As I looked at her and my sister, my heart began to beat rapidly— they were both so beautiful. What a battle this would be. I took a deep calming breath.

My father signaled to two young men standing close by Roseline. Both were tall and handsome and were certainly titled, but I knew neither. Roseline's studies proved successful again as she turned to them and gracefully curtsied, "Lord Stephen. Lord Rupert. Thank you for attending my birthday party."

They both moved to stand as her partner, but Lord Stephen was quicker. The music started and Lord Rupert was left with me. Luckily, he was a good partner who led me well as my feet fought to keep up. I knew I was not particularly graceful, but he kept me from looking a total fool.

"And where are you from, sir?" I politely inquired.

His eyes had been tracking my sister's every move and they stayed there as he answered, "I am the nephew to the King of Alganoun."

"Ah, yes. I have met your good king, the night the Druzazzi attempted to invade our lands some seven years ago." I don't know why I said that. I could see myself attempting to fish out some regard from this man, that it was me who saved the country.

But he did not take the bait. His eyes remained on my sister. "Yes, I was here in your hall that evening as well. Thank the Gods above for our salvation that night."

I wanted to say that no, he should thank me. To say that he was fortunate to be dancing with the lady who had saved their country, that he was probably only alive at this moment due to my actions, but all that came out was, "Indeed."

When the music ended, we were across the ballroom from my father, close to the entrance. I took advantage of the situation and disappeared into the crowd. I could only imagine the thoughts running through my father's head for how to taunt me and I wanted no part of it.

I ended up in the same small room across from the open doors to the Grand Hall that I had been in seven years prior. I don't know why really. While I wanted no more part of the celebration, there was a sick part in me that couldn't stand not knowing what was happening.

I watched as Roseline was the perfected belle of the ball, charming all of her dance partners, garnering the attention of all who beheld her. I watched as Father spoke with many mothers and fathers of the courtiers and imagined how he was wheeling and dealing his daughter's future for his own benefit. And I watched as Father smiled at Roseline. I don't believe he ever realized that I was gone.

At dawn the next morning, I decided to investigate what had happened to Roseline when she was in the forest. She never did tell Mother or me what exactly had transpired. With all that had gone on, there had barely been a moment, so I thought I would find out for myself. Perhaps there had been some calamity in the forest: a fire, possibly a large hunting party that injured many animals. What in the world could have occurred?

I had made a second home of the glen. It was set beside a pristine lake and was very secluded from humans as it was high in the hills and the path to it was relatively hidden and difficult to navigate. I liked being away from humans and their curious stares, their thoughtless comments.

My mother had come here as well when she still retained her powers and it is where Roseline and I would have flown if the Druzazzi had won the battle. There was an ancient storage shed filled with supplies and a well-used fire pit in the center of the glen, all we would have needed to survive.

Since Roseline rarely left the castle, I hoped she had remembered the way here from our childhood. I flew higher and faster, eager to solve the mystery of Roseline's dramatic change.

As I approached from above, I saw an animal lying in the middle of the glen and it wasn't moving! I dropped like a stone and was on the ground in moments, back in my human form and knelt by the body.

It was a beautiful Doe and her body was broken. Her legs, instead of smooth and strong, were bent at odd angles. I listened to her chest and there was just the smallest sound of her beating heart. I let out a gasp as I wasn't sure if I could do it. She was so broken and mangled and so close to death.

But I had to try. I ran my hands along the Doe's beautiful face and whispered into her ear, "It is I, Olive, dear Doe.

I will try my hardest. My very hardest. I promise." With that, I put my hands gently over her heart and I began the chant of healing, "Anhelo Eximo Sano Salus Sanu. Anhelo Eximo Sano Salus Sanu."

The glow started with my hands and then moved up my arms, my chest, until my entire body emitted a greenish glow. I continued to chant, focusing hard, trying to heal this beautiful creature. "Anhelo Eximo Sano Salus Sanu," I continued and then I could start to feel her.

I could feel life flooding from my fingers back into the Doe. I could feel my life force entering her and hers entering mine until our minds were one and then the shock of what happened nearly broke the spell.

The images were so staggering, I had to fight the urge to scream, fight the urge to remove my hands. I gasped and forced myself to continue the chant because I now had the answer to what had happened to Roseline and it was beyond my understanding of what could have been a possibility.

In my mind, I was the Doe and Roseline beckoned to me in her sweet voice holding an apple in her right hand extended towards me. But just as I drew close to take the apple - a slash of metal - I felt a knife pierce my skin, just below my heart. I fell to my knees. I couldn't breathe, there was a horrific burning in my chest.

Roseline knelt over me, grinning happily, "And now, I will heal you, stupid deer." Her hands were on my chest and she was saying the words of healing. I could feel my strength returning. Just when I thought of standing, there was a loud

"Crack!" and my leg exploded in pain. Roseline's smiling face appeared over me again, a hammer in her hand. "Don't worry, I will heal you again."

The nightmare of the Doe continued in my mind as my hands remained on her poor broken body as I chanted and chanted, "Anhelo Eximo Sano Salus Sanu." I could feel the hot tears pouring from my eyes as the deer and I bore her pain, re-lived her memories, but I did not stop. No, I grew stronger and stronger as I chanted and I could feel my life force surging into the deer. Slowly, her legs healed, her wounds closed, until finally she opened her eyes and gazed upon me fully aware again.

"How could she be your sister?" she asked in a quiet voice.

Tears flooded my eyes, "I don't know how she could have done this. I'm so sorry. So very sorry." I put my arms around her and hugged her close.

I hadn't had a chance to think that it was so very odd that there had been no other animals about when I arrived. They were usually eager to greet me, but slowly I became cogni-zant of their presence as they entered the glen.

There were rabbits, squirrels, birds, foxes, moose, and a large buck with two fawns. Their eyes looked at me with fear, something I had never experienced before. And then I heard a growl and a roar and Wolf and Cougar ran into the glen and bared their teeth at me, Bear lumbered behind them growling in frustration as well.

Wolf came forward, "If it were possible, I would have rrrr-ripped her to pieces."

"And I would have helped." Cougar hissed.

It was impossible for an animal to harm a Winnowwood, it was part of our magic. All of the animals knew it, as did Roseline.

"She orrrr-derrred us to leave," growled Bear.

"We had to obey," whispered Buck, as his fawns nervously paced.

The Doe jumped to her feet, ran to her family and nuzzled each of them.

"I don't know what to say." The tears continued to fall down my cheeks, "I could never have imagined that she was capable of this." I looked at them all and could feel their sense of betrayal, "The only thing I can tell you that might give you some comfort is she no longer has her powers as she has winnowed."

Bear growled with delight, "Then I hope to see her soon, as she would make a tasty lunch for us!"

Wolf grinned slyly as well, "Oh, we will be keeping an eye out for her, agrrrr-reeed."

"I hope you will allow *me* to exact her punishment." I asked more than stated.

"If that is your command, Princess, you know we must obey," the Doe replied.

I moved over to her and slowly put my arms around her neck. Her fawns skittered nervously about, worried for their mother. "I am so very sorry."

The Doe looked me in the eye, "She is your sister, she is not you. You are not responsible for what she did."

"I will not let her get away with this." I swore to the Doe.

"All that matters now is you have healed me when I was almost gone and I know you have paid the price for that as well, for you are now far more beautiful than when you arrived."

"Am I?" I walked to the edge of the lake and looked at my reflection in the water. I was prettier. In fact, I was verging on beautiful, "My goodness."

The Doe nuzzled me, "Thank you."

I kissed her velvet nose, "Forgive me." I looked at all of their faces, their apprehension and distrust still showed, "I hope you will all find it in your hearts to trust me again."

∞

If anyone could have seen me, they would have thought it an odd sight for an eagle to cry tears as it flew, but cry I did. Roseline had betrayed the honor of all the Winnowwood. Even if I was the only true one who remained, she betrayed her heritage, all that we stood for, and cast such dishonor on her name.

I knew I had to seek my mother's advice, because at this moment all I longed to do was rip Roseline's beautiful new face into shreds with my razor sharp talons. As I drew near the castle, I didn't have to look far for my mother as she was waving at me from the rose garden, waving rather frantically actually. I flew down, landed on her arm and looked at her. She saw the tears in my eyes.

"Oh, Olive. That was my worst fear." She collapsed onto a stone bench, her hands clasped over her face in sadness.

I changed back into myself and sat down next to her. Mother looked at my face, could see the new damage, then clutched me desperately into her arms, and we cried together.

"The magic must have been very powerful," she sobbed.

My hand went to my face and I could feel the new damage — a large bump over my left eye, a boil next to it, with at least four new large warts clustered next to them. "She spent the day torturing a Doe and then left her for dead."

My mother stiffened in my arms, then pulled back to gaze upon me. "Impossible!" she gasped, "Not my daughter. Not *my* daughter."

"You know I could feel and see all of it." I quietly reminded her, "She stabbed her in the lungs, broke her legs with a hammer, cut her in her neck—"

"No more!" My mother leaped up from the bench, her face wild with despair. She took a deep breath, trying to calm herself, "Were you successful?" she quietly asked.

I went to her, placed my hands into hers, "Yes."

She nodded solemnly, "You are so gifted, my daughter. And you are so good."

I let my hatred for my sister simmer to the surface, "At this moment, I am far from good. At this moment, all I can think of is ripping her beautiful new face from her head!"

"No! You must control yourself. If you hurt your sister, you know what your father will do." She looked down at my left hand, then back into my eyes, "You must not harm her."

"I won't need to, the animals are hunting her," I smugly replied. "They will have their vengeance," I hissed.

My mother's face showed her alarm, "You must stop them!"

An evil laugh came out of me, surprising me with the sound of its malice, "No!"

She put her hands on my face and forced me to look at her, "He will destroy you, if you destroy her!"

I pulled away from her in frustration, hating the truth in her words, "He loves a monster."

Mother sat back down on the bench and sighed, "She's not a monster, Olive. She's just weak, like I was." She began to cry again, "Weak. Weak. Weak."

I sat down next to her, depressed, as reality once again closed in, "I knew all that ever mattered to her was pleasing Father. Why should I be surprised at this? If this was the price that had to be paid for her to achieve her beauty, of course she'd do it."

We sat together in silence for a moment, both knowing that we were the fools in this scheme for not anticipating her actions, not preventing her. I grew angry at myself.

"It's my fault. I was practically gloating to myself over how disappointed she would be when she winnowed. How she was stupid enough to give up her powers and would not be beauti-ful," I sighed in sadness. "I underestimated my sister. I should have known she'd find a way to obtain her heart's desire."

My mother clasped her hands in mine, "I'm so sorry, my darling." She put an arm around me to hold me close, "But you mustn't allow the animals to hurt her."

I sighed, then nodded my agreement. "Your father already has a suitor for her." Mother's face was filled with concern, "I'm worried he's plotting with him to make war against the King of Alganoun."

"He is beyond belief," I was stunned by this news.

She shook her head sadly at me, "At this very moment, Prince Victore sits with Roseline in the palace. He is very handsome, very rich and has hundreds of soldiers at his command."

I sprang up from the bench, "Father is an idiot!" I couldn't hold back, "What is wrong with a man who plots to go to war when there is no cause?"

"As much as Roseline yearned for beauty, your father yearns for power. I fear for our future, I must admit." A deep sadness covered Mother's face, "Please, Olive, do not forsake us." She took me in her arms and hugged me with a desperation that surprised me. "I worry that before this is over, you will have to save us all again."

Roseline was hiding from me. She must have known that I would go to the glen and what I would find there. Then she must be very afraid right now. It made me happy to think that, as I wanted her to fear me, to be in dread of me, filled with terror over what I might to do her. She didn't need to know that I had promised Mother I wouldn't hurt her. I wanted her to think that I would!

SIXTEEN

I had found Victore. I watched as he left with Father to go on a hunt. What they were hunting is certainly a worry, but they had both departed the castle grounds. That left Roseline all to me – my own private hunt at home. I knew she'd be in the castle, as she knew the law and that her life was now forfeit if she left it. How the animals would have their revenge.

Where or where could she be? I changed into a cat, my fur as orange as my hair, and sniffed the air. It wouldn't take me long.

The smell of her rose-scented perfume filled the air and I followed it in a rush – down a long corridor, a left, up a staircase, down a hall to a second staircase, then another long hall that took me to the base of a deserted watchtower. Oh, what have we here? My whiskers flared in the air as I inhaled. This was definitely the place. I cocked my ear and could hear movement in the tower above. I grinned, my cat fangs exposed in an odd, toothy smile.

I stood, my paws in the air, "Anhelo Eximo Lupus Winnowwood," and became the orange-colored killer wolf, then padded silently up the steps to the watchtower.

As I entered the room at the top of the winding staircase, I found her staring out the window with her back to me. She let out a low sigh, "Hello, Sister." She turned around, so beautiful, it still surprised me to look at her. Her eyes begged me for mercy, "I am your sister," she whispered.

I shook my head "no" then let out a long, low growl. I snapped my jaws at her aggressively and moved in, "Grrrrr-rrrrr."

"Would you have preferred if I had hurt more of them? Would that make you happy?" she murmured as she moved away from me, then her hand went to the left side of her face.

Seeing her tell-tale sign of nervousness made me want to scare her all the more. I crouched in my attack position, my ears flat against my head as I growled.

"I am your sister," she declared again. "You *can't* hurt me!" she emphatically added.

I jumped her, knocking her to the ground. I stared at her, my muzzle two-inches from her throat. I opened my jaws and placed my teeth on her cheek then let out another growl, my hot breath pulsating on her bare skin.

"I knew you would find me and I wanted to talk to you alone. That's why I am here. To tell you of Father's plot." She finally begged, "If you don't hurt me, I promise to help you." I let out another long growl. "Father plans to cut your crux off!" she emphatically declared.

I leapt off of her and changed back into myself in an instant. "You must have encouraged him!" I snarled at her.

"I promise I didn't, but it is my fault because I changed." She stood up, striking the dirt off her dress, then smoothed back her hair. "He wants you to become beautiful like Mother and me."

"I. Will. Not." I moved close to her, "I could never, ever, do what you did!"

"I know that. But you must have known that I would." She bravely took my hand, "You know I'm a coward, you've always known that." I looked her in the eye and did not speak.

"If it had been up to me that night when Seagull came, we would all be dead because I would never have found the courage to face Father. I know what I am, Olive, and now, I am happy for I have what I always wanted." She clutched my hands in hers, "But you need to listen to me or you will lose what you love more than anything in this life." She took my left hand into hers and touched my branched finger. "We must keep each other safe, Sister."

I woke up screaming. Again. I bolted upright in my bed, shuddering with fear mixed with relief now knowing it was only a dream. The same dream. The dream I had keep reliving ever since Roseline had told me Father was going to cut off my crux. In my nightmare, I was tied to a chair, unable to lift my arms overhead to transform. Father had the blade in his hand, berating me for my ugliness, for my selfishness in not doing what he wanted and all I could do was cry and beg him for mercy. Every time, my dream ended with him cutting off my finger, but instead of becoming beautiful, I remained as I was – ugly. How he would scream, until my screams melded with his and I would finally wake up, terrified that it was real. I hated living in fear.

4

Eighteen

Four months had passed since Roseline's birthday. We had entered into an uneasy truce; she had changed Father's mind over him removing my crux against my will and I had given her my protection from the animals' fury.

In my heart, I was glad. For in all truth, I couldn't have killed her or allowed the animals to tear her apart. My family may not be perfect, but they are the only family I have. Besides, I've ended up blaming myself for what happened on Roseline's birthday. I should have seen it coming and I failed to pay attention. Roseline is Roseline just as a skunk is a skunk and that is simply the way it is.

I had been completely honest with the Bestiallas and told them of the bargain I had struck. To my great joy, they agreed with me and understood why I now protected Roseline. No animal could harm her unless, of course, I changed my mind.

I was watching her now. We were in our private sitting room and she was busily sketching yet another design for her wedding gown, a happy smile on her lips. She looked up at me, held up her drawing — a gown of red with a dramatic train. "Well?" she waited for my answer.

"Sister, you could wear a gown made of sackcloth and would still be the most beautiful bride anyone has ever beheld," I smiled at her. She grinned her response, satisfied with my answer, and went back to her work.

Last week, I caught her parading about with Mama's crown on her head, practicing waving to a crowd only she could see. I had snuck out of the room before she noticed I was there and left her to it. I just don't get it, why is this so amusing to her? Is this all she would demand from her life? To be a beautiful peacock preening for the approval from the crowd? I had never seen her happier and she showed no remorse over her decision to give up her powers. I truly could not understand it. If I lost my powers, I would no longer know what my existence in this world could be. Sometimes I wondered how we could be sisters, but then I remembered all of my previous Winnowwood sisters had made the same choice as Roseline. I had to face it — I was the odd one and now the only one left. I looked down at my crux and gently touched it. It was everything to me.

Roseline held up her drawing again, the train now longer and even more dramatic, "I will look so beautiful when I marry Victore!" she giggled with delight. "Slippers! What kind of slippers shall I wear with my gown?" I know she didn't expect me to answer, she knew I knew nothing of fashion. A new piece of papers and she began sketching what looked like a jeweled pair of red slippers.

Roseline is ridiculously head-over-heels in love with Victore. She practically purrs at any comment he makes, completely enraptured with the dull stories of his "so called" exploits. I have a feeling that less than half of anything he has told her is true for he doesn't strike me as a man of true courage. He lacks that strength of character. I don't mean to sound harsh, but few people surprise me. I've learned how to observe too well and there is emptiness in him that scares me. People who are empty in spirit are dangerous – look at my father.

At dinner that night, I watched my sister smiling brightly at her beloved. Her incessant giggles truly drive me crazy – is this how one must act to gain a husband? If so, I am in serious trouble for all of her actions seem so foreign to me. I'll just hope it's her who's the crazy one and the world is not this insane, but of late I've begun to hear this little mocking voice inside my head chiding me. It whispers, "Your sister is not the crazy one." I hate that little voice and do my best to ignore it.

But I do know I'm right about Victore and I will find him out, it will just take a little patience. I watched him closely as he manipulated my family. I watched him as he prepared for his assault, then found his opening when my father mentioned hearing of a mysterious bandit named Black Bart. He smiled a warm sneer at my father and all I could think of is how a snake looks at a fat mouse right before it springs.

"The country is falling to pieces! Highwaymen have almost taken over all of our trade routes and what does the King of Alganoun do?" Victore arched an eyebrow toward my father.

"He doesn't deserve to wear his crown when he will not protect his own people!" Then my father eagerly added, "I would not have it so in my kingdom."

"Exactly." He offered another nod of affirmation to my father, "Black Bart runs rampant throughout the kingdom, taking travelers unaware, stealing all they have," he paused for effect, "There are rumors he is even in cahoots with the Druzazzi."

I felt my heart skip a beat and I stopped breathing. But as I watched Victore and looked into his eyes, there was something there that made me think he was lying.

Roseline gasped with fear, "You must find him and kill him!"

He placed his hand on top of Roseline's, "Don't worry my darling girl, I will never let any harm come to you."

She looked at him, then let out a sigh that could only be expressed as the sound of love. She was such an idiot.

The next day, I overheard Victore tell Roseline he was going for a ride. He asked her to go with him, but she refused. I think she's still nervous that one of the animals might rip her to shreds. As if I couldn't control them!

I decided that I would go riding with him, only I would run in the forest behind him and spy on what he did. I'd just go in a different form. After all, someone has to protect the family.

I followed cautiously, my hooves meeting his mount's pace. He seemed nervous initially, stopping and listening for any sound of followers, his eyes searching the sky. Somehow I knew he was looking for me. I engaged the help of a seagull, who flew high overhead as a beacon for me to follow Victore's path. If Roseline had told him all about me, he would know I would be an orange-colored bird and not be wary of a simple seagull.

Once he felt secure that I wasn't following him, he rose hastily through the forest, later taking the shortcut to the sea through Buckmeade Pass. I paused at the pass's entrance and waited for Seagull's signal before I entered the graveyard of the Druzazzi. There were no remnants of any bodies, no discarded weapons or clothing, yet, to walk through the canyon of the pass sent shivers down my spine. It was as if I could feel their ghosts as I rode through them. The memories of that night began to fill me so I decided to run. I knew I was being foolish, but it just felt like evil surrounded me and needed to get away from it as fast as I could.

As I made my way safely out of the canyon, I saw Victore approaching the bluffs in front of the shoreline. I moved to the edge of the forest as he rode his horse up a high bluff overlooking the beach. He stared out at the ocean as if he was expecting to see something appear, but there was nothing on the horizon.

I gazed intently upon his face. It was almost as if he was deciding something, his face serious, contemplative. Then, he suddenly laughed. It was all so bizarre. He laughed again and thrust his fist into the sky. I could almost see him grow in stature as he was so full of himself.

How I wish I could have read his thoughts. The hair on my back stood up, something was wrong. I could feel it in my soul. I watched the look on his face and I knew – he was planning something treacherous.

My birthday had dawned bright and beautiful. An hour after sunrise, I flew to the glen to see my friends. It was already official. As soon as the dawn had broken, I had reached the age where my daughters would be born as Winnowwoods. Tonight's ceremony would be a mere formality. The future, if there was a future for the Winnowwood, would rely on me. I have to admit, it felt rather overwhelming.

As I flew, a thought crossed my mind – I had spent my life focused on getting to this day with my crux intact, but I had rarely given a thought as to who would father my daughters? Who would be my spouse? That was a sobering notion. I had completely avoided thinking of men, as I knew how they wanted to avoid me – running from rejection before I could be rejected.

In the days before the blade, the Winnowwood captured unsuspecting men in the forest and forced them to drink a potion that made the men think the women were beautiful and then the men happily mated with them. When they awoke alone in the forest, all they remembered was mating with a beautiful woman. Needless to say, it was easy to find unsuspecting men in the forest.

The first time my mother told me the story, I couldn't believe it, but she said it had gone on for centuries. The immorality of drugging those men stung me and I was ashamed of my people, but my mother only laughed at me when I voiced my concerns. "How have we harmed them, Olive?" she let out a snicker. "We did not force ourselves on them. We did not take their choice away. We just created an illusion that they acted upon. They only remember the joy of the union with a beautiful woman, which is what they long for. Would you have our line made extinct instead? We owe our very existence to them and what they did." I admit that it seemed a worthwhile bargain when she put it that way.

I wondered if I would ever find anyone willing to be my mate and that irritating small voice inside said, "No". That same voice again told me my sister was not so stupid after all. I was really beginning to hate that little voice! I wouldn't even know how to concoct a magical potion that would make a man think I was beautiful. But then I thought of how my mother and father had met.

It was the only story I ever loved of my father. Though my mother rarely spoke of it, one day when Roseline and I were both quite small, she told us of how Father had fallen in love with her before she had winnowed — that it was true love. She had told us all of it with tears in her eyes. I loved thinking of that story whenever my father was cruel to me, for it made me think that at one time, he must have been different for he had seen my mother's true beauty. It bothered me that she had not become beautiful before she winnowed like the legend had said, so I always figured that part of the legend had just been a lie, fabricated by that old witch.

My mother's story gave me a perverse sense of hope for myself when I thought of it, for if a man like my father could see my mother's true beauty, then surely there must be hope for me. Perhaps I wouldn't have to give them a magical potion to mate with me. I smiled to myself as I thought of it.

As I flew over the glen, I let out a "Shrrreee" of happiness. I could see the meadow was crowded with my friends to celebrate with me. As I landed and changed back into my human form, eighteen hummingbirds, carrying a delicate crown of flowers, placed it on my head as everyone sang the birthday song to me.

Hark for our high priestess is among us,
Marking eighteen years today.
This Winnowwood has joined her sisters,
She will be brave and courageous we pray.
The lineage of her daughters now guaranteed,
Princess of the Winnowwood so blessed on her birthday.
The Bestiallas now yours to command,
To you, our high priestess, our love and devotion always.

It was so lovely, it brought tears to my eyes. I had longed for this day for so many years and I finally realized what it meant as I looked at them as they sang this beloved song. They were mine, and I was theirs, forever. I would never be alone. If I were lucky, I would live to be hundreds of years old.

The first to greet me was the Doe I had saved. She pushed her velvety nose against by cheek, "The Last of the Winnowwood, it is to you fair Olive that the Bestiallas gives our allegiance and our hopes and prayers for your happiness. Today, all the animals of the world pledge their devotion to you."

Her Buck behind her added his good wishes, "May you never winnow. May your heart be courageous and your will unwavering."

Bear added his thoughts for the day, "We know it may seem self-serving, but we wish you courage to remain as you are, faithful to your ancestors. Yet, we also know what is in your heart. Since you were a little girl, you have always been the bravest of any Winnowwood we have ever known. The legend is for you, dear Olive. One day, a Prince will see your heart and will love you for who you are."

I hugged his neck, "Oh Bear, who would have thought you a sentimental believer in that ancient legend? That was just a lie by that awful witch to torment us all the more."

"My ancestor was there at that lake. He heard the spell and it has been recited from mother to cub for four hundred years. I am not sentimental," he let out a small, irritated growl, then rose up on his hind legs and in a thunderous voice spoke, "Curse you ugly wretches! With beauty! Cut it off in the moonlight, but no more magic, unless she is loved warts and all!"

With a look of deep satisfaction on his face, he sat down. "I repeat the truth. One day, all the world will see it come to pass. This I do know."

His words were spoken with such assurance that it made me want to believe in them as well. "Then I shall hope that Prince you speak of has terrible eyesight," I smiled at him.

He looked me in the eye, "His eyes will be clear and his heart as true as yours."

I thought of my worries about finding my future mate and felt the beginning of tears in my eyes. I reached out and put my hand on his furry cheek, "May it be as you say, dear friend, if only to give me hope."

A mother Rabbit stood nervously to the side, her leg thumped in a jerking motion. I knelt down beside her. "Rabbit, what ails you?"

Her whiskers nervously twitched as she looked up at me, "I'm sorry, Princess, but my boy was on the cliffs overlooking the valley this morning when the sun came up. He saw something that you need to hear about. It's not good." With that she gave the little bunny a push forward. He looked up at me, his eyes bulging, his nose trembling.

I sat down next to him on the grass, then picked him up and stroked his head. "Dear Bunny, there's no need to be nervous. You know I'm your friend. Whatever you saw, it cannot be so terrible."

"S-soldiers. In the valley," he finally stammered.

My breath caught in my throat and for a few moments I forgot to breathe. "Could you describe them? Did they have white hair?" I tried to keep my voice calm, even if I felt like screaming.

He shook his head back and forth, "No, they wore metal suits with yellow ribbons on their horses."

As much as it filled me with relief to know it was not the Druzazzi, my fear was not unfounded as these had to be my father's men. "Were there many soldiers?" I asked.

The Bunny looked perplexed. He looked at his toes, at his paws, attempting to count, but got lost. He looked about the glen, hundreds of animals were roaming about. "More than us," he declared.

I gazed out at all of the animals, there had to be over a thousand crowding the glen, "A lot more?"

He looked about nervously, then bobbed his head, "Yes, Princess."

I could feel my shoulders slump, "Were *all* of the soldiers in yellow?" The Bunny nodded again. I wondered how my father had managed it. Did my Mother know? I was certain Victore must have had a hand in this, but I was unsure as to how. I would find that out as soon as possible.

I patted the Bunny, then stood, "I suppose I'd better go back to the castle and see what has happened." Of course he'd do this on my birthday, I thought to myself. I wondered if he was with the soldiers.

The animals crowded around me and gave me their last well-wishes, as I quickly hugged and greeted them. "Thank you for this. I love you all so very much."

When I returned, I went to the dining room, as it was our family tradition to celebrate Birthday Luncheon together. Mother and I were still vegetarians, but since Roseline's change, she had also changed her eating habits — steak was now on the menu. I couldn't stand to watch her eat meat, but of course it had pleased Father to have another carnivore at the table. Today, only my favorite dishes would be served, so there would certainly not be any animals on the menu.

Only Mother and Roseline were there to greet me when I arrived. Both looked like they had a secret and from the looks on their faces, it wasn't a good one. Needless to say, I probably had the bigger secret as to what Father was up to and I wasn't telling as he was probably on his way to attack the King of Alganoun.

"Good morning." I spoke with as much cheer as I could rally given those looks.

Mother smiled and moved quickly to me and gave me a big hug, "Happy Birthday, my darling girl," then kissed me on my cheek.

Roseline hugged me as well, "Happy Birthday, dear Sister."

"What's the matter?" I looked quizzically at them both.

"It's nothing, my dear," my mother said softly.

Roseline looked at her, "Just tell her the truth. Olive doesn't want to hear lies, especially today."

Mother looked from Roseline to me, "You're Father has left the castle. He said he would not return until tomorrow."

"Did he forget it was my birthday?" I quietly asked.

"No." my mother whispered, "He said he is tired of you defying him and he has refused to attend."

I could feel my face flush; my pulse began to beat faster. Is this how much he hates me? Could he truly despise me so? One of the most important moments in my life and he refuses to attend? He'd rather declare war on this day than attend my celebration – it was like he declared war on me. Again.

I walked to the window, turning my back to them so they couldn't see my face. It was hard not to cry, I blinked my eyes furiously as I looked out through their blur to the sky outside. Part of me just wanted to change and fly away, but I didn't want to be a coward, "Will Greatpapa be here?" I tried to keep my voice steady.

"Yes, of course." My mother came up behind me and placed her arm around my waist.

"Probably best that only the people who actually love me will be here." I flashed what I hoped passed for a smile at my mother and sister. They obviously didn't know how many soldiers had accompanied Father when he had left the castle on his pre-dawn expedition, but there was nothing to be done about it for now.

I wouldn't let him ruin my day any more than he already had. I refused to think about him another moment and tried not to think about what mission he was really on instead of being here for my celebration. I just prayed that no one would die, not today.

"Are you alright?" Roseline's concerned face stared at me, her hand gently touched my cheek.

I tried to focus on the moment and not to think of Father. "Yes, dear Sister." I looked into her eyes and smiled, "I have waited for this day for so many years." I held out my hand and looked at my crux, "I want to celebrate that one day my daughters will be Winnowwoods and I know I have you to thank for helping me reach this day."

Roseline put her arms around me, "Even if we look at the world somewhat differently," she kissed me on my cheek, "I am so proud to call you Sister."

I looked at her beautiful face, then kissed her on the cheek as well, "And I you."

Under the light of the moon, we stood: Greatpapa, Roseline, Mother and me. I wore an exquisite green gown Greatpapa had given me for my birthday. It had once been my grandmother's and it was stunning. I swear I felt more powerful in it, as if somehow a bit of her magic still lingered in its cloth.

Again my mother wore the white silk robe of the high priestess, the embroidered silver stitches gleaming in the moonlight. Now that I was of age, that robe would be mine since Mother no longer had her powers. Mother somberly lit eighteen candles held in tall iron sconces that encircled us as she chanted an ancient incantation.

She motioned to me, and I knelt in front of her on an embroidered silver carpet. She laid her hands upon my head and blessed me. "Great Mother, bless this brave young woman who is the last of us who holds your blood, the last to bear your gifts. Let your goodness bless her with daughters who will follow in all your ways. Show her your magic, reveal your power, and lead her to use her powers for good. Let her way be blessed by you as you guide her on her journey. Great Mother, protect her from the evil ones who will cross her path and give her your strength and courage to reign over her foes."

Those may sound like simple words, but I felt a new power surge through me. I felt like my grandmother was with me, though I had never even met her. I don't know how confidence can be transmitted through a blessing, but that's how I felt — like I could do anything, that I was blessed, that I would have the courage to face any enemy.

My mother took my hands into hers and guided me to my feet. "Behold Olive, Last of the Winnowwood!" She then bowed before me, as did my sister and my Greatpapa.

Without warning, a squire burst into the small court-yard, "Your Grace, the King has been captured by the King of Alganoun!" It would seem that Father was set on ruining my birthday.

5

Prisoner

High in the air, I tucked my head and plummeted downwards, the air rippling over my wings, hurtling towards Alganoun Castle. Faster, as I screamed past windows, racing, as the ground rose up before me until I propelled myself upwards again at last. I spied a turret set in the middle of the castle – the perfect place. I winged quickly towards it, then past a window in the turret and caught a glimpse of Father. Turning swiftly in the air, I landed on the edge of the window and kept out of sight.

There was a short man standing in front of Father holding out a scroll. It was the King of Alganoun, I remembered his face from before.

My father stared arrogantly down at him, his mouth as petulant as an unhappy child's. I hoped he would get what he deserved. Certainly I didn't want him to die, but I was almost glad he had been bested for behaving like such a fool.

Was Victore here? Perhaps he had been captured as well and was being held in a separate cell? Something inside of me said no, like a warning, like this was a clue as to what was going to happen next.

King Ivan held out the scroll towards Father, "As we discussed," he stated firmly.

My father looked down his nose at him, "You should have been my prisoner."

Does this man know no end to his self-importance? I almost shuddered with embarrassment as I spied on them. King Ivan seemed unperturbed, "Suffice to say, this is your only option now. Do you accept?" King Ivan took a candle from the table and melted sealing wax onto the scroll.

My father's face was filled with anger when he finally spoke, "For my daughter!" With that, he slammed his gold signet ring into the hot wax.

Well, I knew what daughter he was referring to and it certainly wasn't me. He must have forced my father into some sort of alliance. The King had a son a few years older than me. Could my father have given him Roseline? If so, her anger would be limitless. I almost laughed, it would be a new experience to have her as the one angry with Father for once. Indeed, it might be best if he remained a prisoner to protect him from Roseline's wrath.

King Ivan handed the scroll to a knight in armor and I caught a glimpse of his face. It was Lord Rupert; the one I had danced with just four short months ago.

"Deliver this at once to Queen Opal. Let her know her husband is safe," he paused as he looked to my father, "For now. She must abide by the terms."

Lord Rupert took the scroll from the King, "Yes, your Grace." He bowed, then quickly left the room.

King Ivan moved towards the window, so I took off. I was far in the sky above him before he looked out.

From high overhead, I tracked Rupert as he rode his war horse across the countryside. Peasants, harvesting the wheat in the fields, dove for cover when they heard his approach and hid themselves until he thundered past. They must be filled with fear, worried another war was upon them. I sighed as I thought of Father's actions, bringing this to our doorstep through his own arrogance and foolishness.

Below me, Rupert rode through a grove of oak trees, its canopy of fall leaves hiding him from my sight. I circled above waiting for him to reappear. But he didn't. Perhaps he was answering the call of nature and I certainly didn't want to see that. I continued to circle until curiosity got the best of me and then I flew down to investigate.

Landing high in one of the oak trees, I peered down and saw four men in hooded cloaks on the ground below, the short one was securing Rupert's saddlebag to his horse. Rupert lay on the ground, unmoving, the visor to his helmet was open, but his eyes were shut. He didn't look dead, as there were no marks on his armor or body, but he did appear unconscious. Then I noticed a rope tied to a tree discarded to the side. They must have used it to knock him off his horse.

The tallest man spoke, "And that's why we're the best highwaymen in the land!" he said in a lilting tone.

Another husky-looking fellow with a mustache joined in, "Feared by all, and rightly so..."

"...for we'll kill you just for show, ho, ho!" a young voice added his part.

The short man turned to him, "Never for show, Puntalo."

I could tell by the tone of his voice and how the other three reacted that this must be their leader.

The young man named Puntalo seemed embarrassed, "Of course, Bart."

Bart!? Was this the notorious highwayman Victore had spoken of at dinner? I couldn't make out his face, the hood of his cloak prevented it. So, they robbed Rupert. I wondered what they had stolen.

As I watched them from my high perch, they began to climb up into the trees. Bart looked up and I caught a glimpse of his face — it wasn't a handsome face, not even by a mother's definition, but it didn't look as cruel as his reputation dictated either. Could this man be in cahoots with the Druzazzi as Victore implied?

Once they were high in the trees hidden by its canopy, Puntalo sprinkled drops of water from his canteen down onto Rupert's face. He awoke with a start. His hand went to his head and clanked against the metal. He pulled off his helmet and furiously rubbed what I assumed was a lump on the back of his head. His face froze for a moment as if he had thought of something important, he clambered to his feet then frantically opened his saddlebag. I could see his relief when he pulled out the scroll that King Ivan had given him, the seal still intact. He remounted his horse, then road away.

The tall man snickered from below, "Probably thinks it was the hand of God that knocked him off his horse."

Then the one with the mustache spoke, "Terribly clever of you, if I do say so myself. Rather fiendish, I daresay."

I recognized Bart's voice as he spoke, "Yes. The games begin again, and I shall win as I always do."

The taller man spoke again, "It's for the best though."

Bart began to clamber back down the tree, "Yes, it is. Now everything will be played by my hand instead of the King's." They jumped down to the ground and quickly disappeared into a thicket of trees.

What did he mean by that? And which King? Had something happened before I had arrived, did I miss something significant? I couldn't decide what to do for a moment, continue following Rupert or chase after this Black Bart?

Probably best if I stay with Rupert I decided, in case these bandits had done something as they seemed to think they had. I needed to figure out what the mystery was. I took off. When I was high in the sky, I spied Rupert, who was almost to Rosemount Castle. I glanced back to the bandits and spotted them on horses heading to the southwest. Perhaps I would be able to find them later.

If you had never seen our castle, your first glimpse would make quite a first impression as it is so striking. The castle's massive walls are covered in an explosion of colors made up of magical roses, which climb the walls to the top of the turrets. The yellow banners of our sigil ripple in the breeze: a red rose on a field of yellow. I think that it looks like a living painting by a master artist. Whenever I'm troubled, I stand on the highest turret and just breathe, it always helps me find myself again.

I floated lower in the sky so I could watch Rupert closely as he arrived at the gate.

Rupert jerked his horse to a stop, barely in time to prevent running over our guard.

The guard of the watch stepped forward, "Identify yourself, sir!"

He lifted his face plate and glared arrogantly down at the guard, "I am Lord Rupert of Alganoun, you fool. I have an important message for Queen Opal from King Michael."

The guard was momentarily taken aback, then almost whispered his reply, "Then the King lives?"

"For now," replied Rupert condescendingly, "Out of my way!"

The guard jumped back, just avoiding Rupert's horse mowing him down. I was thinking a great deal less of Rupert as I watched him in action. I despised mean people.

∾

I stood in the shadows of an alcove to the side of the throne room and scrutinized Rupert's face as he stared at my mother. As with any male who gazed upon her, I think if she told him to jump out the window at that very moment he would do it with a smile on his lips. Mother may not have her magical powers anymore, but she certainly still wielded power. She sat on her throne, carefully reading the scroll Rupert had delivered.

Rupert stared unabashedly at her. I could only imagine what he was thinking, as he had a silly little smirk on his face.

Roseline had remained in our sitting room, she had no idea what I suspected was in this scroll and I had encouraged her to stay there working on her latest wedding gown design. I couldn't imagine what would happen when Mother broke the news to her.

Mother finally looked up at Rupert, "Are you aware of the contents of this message, sir?"

Rupert looked almost dazed as he attempted to form a reply. I really have to stop underestimating the power of my mother and sister.

"Speak, sir," my mother demanded.

Rupert found his tongue at last, "Indeed I am, your majesty. King Michael signed it in my presence."

My mother's face filled with concern, "You are certain these are *his* wishes?"

Rupert pointed to the gold seal on the parchment, "As you can see by his seal."

She examined the seal closely, her fingers tracing the emblem, "Yes, it is his seal." She bit her lip, concerned over the contents and I knew I was right. He had traded Roseline. "You may go, sir. I shall comply with my husband's request."

Rupert looked relieved, "Will the Princess be ready to begin her journey in a fortnight?"

My mother stared at him alarmed, "I thought you were aware of the contents?" Rupert nodded his head. My mother began to speak to him like she was speaking to a child, "The journey is to begin in the morning." She sighed, "I do hope your ability to find your way home outpaces your memory."

I studied Rupert's face, he looked completely confused. He babbled his response, "Uh, yes, your Grace," his face flushed red.

That set off an alarm for me. What had that highwayman done? Rupert was confused and too embarrassed to tell my mother. What part of his plot was he now manipulating? My apprehension continued to grow, I had to figure out what was happening.

❧

My sister's shrieking surely awakened my ancestors from their crypts. "He can't, Mother! He just can't! He knows I love Victore. Why, oh why, would he do this to me?" Roseline was filled with rage, but her eyes were filled with tears.

Mother put her arms around her and held her close, "I know, my love. I know," she gently whispered, stoking her hair.

"No, you don't know!" she screamed as she pulled away, then stomped about the room flailing her arms in frustration. She stopped and pointed at Mother. "YOU married a handsome Prince! And instead of Victore, my beautiful, darling Victore, who I *adore*, you want me to marry this cretin!"

She grabbed one of my books off the table and hurled it across the room. I ran to it and picked it up, gently brushing it off. This was my favorite book, "Animals of the World". My Greatpapa had given it to me when I turned twelve and it was one of my prized possessions. I decided to hold onto it until she had calmed down as she continued to scream.

"An ugly frog of a man who is our sworn enemy! I do not deserve such a match. Not ME. Not *me*, Mother!" This time Roseline stomped both her feet for good measure.

Mother lost her patience at last and grabbed Roseline hard by her shoulders, "Roseline, understand this – our very future is at stake. They will kill your father! They could kill us. This marriage will seal the peace between our countries…" she looked her square in the eye, "…you must do your duty."

She jerked away from Mother, turned towards me looking like she was going to start screaming again at the top of her lungs. Instead, she threw herself into my arms and began to cry like a child. I dropped my book and had to steady us both as I hadn't expected her to do that.

"Oh, Olive, please don't let them do this to me. I beg you, please, help me, dear Sister. I know you will find a way…" she continued to sob and murmur, "…help me," as I held her in my arms.

I looked at Mother, her face was filled with pain as well. She certainly didn't want to force Roseline into this match.

An idea formed in my mind, "I know where Father is being held. I could go instead of Roseline. Once I was in the castle, I'm sure I could rescue him."

Roseline looked at me puzzled, "But Father asked for his "beautiful" daughter. If you'd only winnow…"

"NO!" I sprang away from her as if she'd slapped me. "How could you think I would do that?" I glared at her, furious over her suggestion as to how to solve her problem.

"But I *love* Victore," she whined, "You can't take away my happiness!"

"But you would kill me to get it!" my voice sliced the air.

Roseline looked at me and knew I'd never do what she asked. She collapsed into a chair defeated, and began to sob all the louder.

I looked at Mother, "I will try to rescue him, that much I will do for Roseline."

She frowned, "Your plan sounds dangerous. I won't let you put yourself in peril."

Roseline choked back her sob and wiped her eyes, "But you'll make me marry him and end my happiness without a moment's hesitation." She turned to me, pleading, "Tell us of your plan, dear Sister."

～

At dawn the next morning, I stood on the highest turret of the castle smelling the delicious scent of the roses mixed with the early morning dew. It calmed me. I hadn't slept well. It wasn't my usual nightmare, instead my dreams had been filled with darkness and images of war. Something in me knew Victore was behind Father's capture, but I hadn't found the connection. Still, as I looked out over the countryside, I knew what I had to do, so I jumped.

I fell like a rock hurtling towards the ground below, then lifted my arms over my head and called out, "Anhelo Eximo Aquila Winnowwood!" and changed into my eagle form, flapped my wings and soared into the air, missing the ground by a good twenty-feet. Mother cringed whenever she saw me do this and begged me to stop, but I thought it was thrilling.

Streaking through the sky, I made my way to the glen. "Shree! Shree!" I called to the Bestiallas. By the time I had changed into my human form, they were gathering, as anxious as I was because I had already told them — war was coming.

I waited until everyone had assembled. Most nervously paced, waiting to hear the final decision. Bear was sitting next to me, he had a look of paternal concern and I knew he would worry for me once he heard my plan.

"All is now in place to rescue my father," I paused briefly before I continued, "I will leave today."

"Grrrr-eat," growled Wolf, "I'll enjoy hunting down any-one who gets in our way."

"Agr-rrreed," added Bear, "Let us take the lead. We will find your father for you," he looked at me with his soft, brown eyes.

I knew he was trying to protect me. I reached out and placed my hand on his cheek, "Actually, I was hoping to avoid a battle."

Bear's ears went down in disappointment. Wolf let out a low growl of displeasure.

"Don't be downcast, my friends, before this is over, I have a terrible feeling that we will all have to fight."

Doe moved forward, "What do you fear, Princess?"

"I wish I knew."

"But how will you rescue your father?" Bear asked.

74

"My father has made a pact with the King of Alganoun to end the war and have his beautiful daughter marry his son. I will leave today."

For a moment none of them spoke. Bear look defeated, "You're going to winnow," he quietly stated. A cacophony of protest erupted, "No!" "Please, don't." "You can't winnow!"

I held up my hand for silence, then smiled at them, "I have no intention of winnowing!" They quieted down, relieved, "Have faith my friends, I will never abandon you."

"I'm sorry I doubted you," Bear looked at me troubled, "But how will you do this?"

"I will simply wear a thick veil and pretend I'm my sister. None of them will doubt me. If I need your help, I will send for you," I put my arms around him and gave him a hug, "It should be a simple thing."

"May it be as you say," he softly replied, "but careful, Princess. Look how easily they captured your father."

"True. I still haven't figured out how they were able to so cleverly ambush him. It was as if King Ivan's army appeared from out of nowhere. There was barely a battle," I turned, frustrated.

"It was Prince Vic-torrrrre, he was not ther-rrre," Wolf growled.

"And I'd love to know where he was. Has anyone seen Victore?" I asked.

A bluebird peeped, "In the forest, by the sea."

I let out a sigh, why my father let Victore talk him into such a foolish act: warring against the King of Alganoun. "I will find him after I rescue my father, I suppose we'll need his help." I turned when I heard an angry voice and saw a large fox pushing a smaller fox away from him and the others.

"Sit over there," the big fox demanded, "We don't want you next to us, you ugly side stripe. You don't even look like a proper fox!" He gave the fox a sharp shove and he tumbled over in a ball.

I watched as the little fox, who did possess a rather odd stripe on his face, slowly crawled away — alone. I strode over and scooped him up in my arm, "That is a rather remarkable stripe. I think I shall call you Side Stripe. Would that be alright?"

The little fox beamed with delight and nodded his head, but just as he was about to speak, I heard another sound — a whimper of pain. I turned.

There was Cougar entering the glen, carrying her cub gently by the scruff of his neck. I quickly placed the fox cub on the ground and moved over to her.

She put her cub gently down in front of me, exhausted. It was covered in blood, a pierce mark in his back. "What happened?" I asked.

Cougar panted hard, "We...we were out hunting. The men came. They had spears. Their dogs almost had us," Cougar glared at Wolf, who hung his head in shame, embarrassed by his distant relatives' actions. She looked back to me pleading, "Can you help him, Princess? Please, please help him."

I sat down and brought the cub close into my arms, then placed my hands gently over his injury. "Anhelo Eximo Salus Sanu," I spoke as I began my chant. The greenish glow appeared on my hands and crept up my arms, my neck and over my face until even the strands of my hair luminesced with the green light. I could feel my power enter the little cub and I could see the hunting scene in my mind as the dogs chased them, as the spear entered him, I continued to chant. I could feel Cougar carrying me, running through the forest, evading the dogs, exhausted. Finally, I could feel the little cub's wound closing under my hands and then he began to purr. I removed my hands and I was myself.

I looked over to Cougar, "You are so brave, my friend, and such a good mother." I scratched the ears of the cub as he stretched out extended, still purring.

Cougar nuzzled my neck, "Thank you, dear Princess."

I placed the cub next to her, then stood, "I suppose I'd better head back," I glanced up at the sun, higher in the sky than it should have been and I knew they'd be waiting for me. "I'll either return or send a messenger when the time comes." I looked over to Bear, "You know where Alganoun Castle stands?"

"Who-ooo could miss it?" Owl answered from the tree.

"Then I'm sure I shall see you soon," I stood and extended my arms over my head, "Anhelo Eximo Aquila Winnowwood!" and flew high into the sky. Who knows how my plan would work out? I pushed away my feelings of impending doom and pushed higher into the sky.

6

Betrayed

I made it home in record time knowing I was late and that my mother would be anxious. I spotted her at her window with a look of apprehension on her face. She smiled when she spied me, then stepped back as I drew close and flew into her room.

"I wondered what was keeping you," she turned to me as I changed back into myself. A look of concern flashed across her face, "What happened?" She moved quickly to my side, examining the new damage on my face.

"Cougar's cub was hurt. It was fortunate I was there." I stared into her green eyes, my eyes, the only part of me that reflected our shared heritage.

"And you are all the more plain for it," Mother sighed in response. "Sometimes I worry that I've encouraged you too much. Perhaps I should have urged you to be more like your sister."

"What!" I looked at her in shock.

"It's just this plan of yours..." her face was filled with sadness, "...I'm so worried for you, Olive. If you're caught, I couldn't forgive myself for putting you in such danger." Tears filled her eyes.

I took her hand into mine, "Mama, they will not catch me." I touched her cheek and smiled, "You know I'm far too clever for that."

"I thought I was too clever once as well, yet, here I stand before you – powerless, a shell of who I wanted to be." She turned from me, her voice grew quiet, "Sometimes in this life, we must do the unthinkable." With that, she took a deep breath and walked quickly to her dresser and opened an intricately decorated wooden box.

A shudder ran down my spine, I knew what that box contained, "NO!" She removed the Blade of the Winnowwood and turned to me. "Mother, I do not choose it! I DO NOT WANT IT! You promised me!" I screamed at her.

Mother held up her hand to silence me, a look of steel in her eyes that I found frightening. I was astounded at her action, she had always been there for me, yet, she now held the blade in her hand – the blade that represented all of the evilness in the world to me. I sat down on the divan, my knees weak from the confusion I felt.

She sat down next to me, the blade wrapped tightly in her left hand. "If you fail and are captured, you could still save our country: become beautiful, marry the Prince.

"No." I whispered my reply.

"My dear daughter," she took my hand into hers. I felt numb so I let her. "I fear I have misled you. I learned this lesson the hard way and it appears you must as well: For a woman, it is beauty and only beauty that is worshipped."

I clasped my hand too tightly around hers, squeezing it in utter desperation, "Then I choose not to be worshipped. If that is all a man can see, then I choose to be ignored!" I hissed at her.

A tear crept down my mother's beautiful face, "I thought that too once." She looked down at the round white scar on her finger. "It was very hard for me to give up, Olive. I was just a year older than you are now when I winnowed." She paused, biting on her lip, but a look of resolve filled her face, "But I must tell you the truth before you go." She jerked to a stand, then moved to the window and in a shaking voice continued her confession, "When it was decided that I would marry your father, I had not yet winnowed."

"I know, he loved you for who you were. It's the only thing that I have ever respected about Father." And one I found surprising no matter how many times I reflected on it.

Mother's shoulders slumped further, her head down, not meeting my eyes. "You know that the legend states that if a Prince would love a Winnowwood, who had not yet changed, but he could see the beauty in her heart, her true beauty would be revealed and she would retain her winnowing powers. I could not imagine giving up my powers," she glanced up, meeting my eyes at last.

I nodded my agreement and she continued, "I so hoped he would love me as I was...then I met him. He was so handsome, Olive. He tried to hide his repulsion of me, but..." She turned away from me and faced the wall, "...It was obvious I disgusted him. He apologized and retreated to his rooms." She turned back towards me and with a firm voice continued, "That night, under the light of the moon, my father assisted me and I chose the winnowing."

She unsheathed the knife. The way the morning light lit the ruby blade in its rays almost made the blade appear alive – throbbing in the light – glistening, sparkling – the red blade glimmering ominously. "The next morning when he happened upon me in the garden, he immediately fell to his knees and professed his eternal love and devotion." She looked away and couldn't meet my eyes.

To say I was overwhelmed with this news is beyond understatement. I had built my life, my very future, on the story she had told me as a child. "But I thought...you said... you *said* that it was true love!"

She walked over to me, anger and betrayal in her voice, "The legend is a lie. A lie not to be thought real." She knelt down, grabbed my hand and moved it to her beautiful face, "This is real."

"Why did you lie to me? I always thought he saw you for your true beauty!" I snapped angrily, grabbing my hand away from her face, then jumped up from my seat and glared down at her.

My mother's face was filled with embarrassment as she searched for her excuse. "I did my duty for my father and the future of my family." She stroked the scar on her hand, "I know it was wrong of me to paint it so romantically. Look at Roseline and her stubborn, willful refusal to do her duty now." She finally met my gaze, "This is entirely my fault. I know that. I admit that, Olive."

I couldn't bear the news, I could feel the heat lighting my face in anger, "I despise Father even more after this revelation. I had thought at one time, he must have been..." I worked hard to form the word, "...kind." I let out a long gasp of pain as my heart broke. "At least now I understand why you lost your powers. I thought the legend must have been a lie," I turned and faced her, "but it was you who lied!" I couldn't stop it any longer, the tears sprang from my eyes and I collapsed into a chair sobbing.

Mother shook her head in irritation, "Oh Daughter, don't be so naïve! He was a Prince. Why should he settle for the ugly daughter of a Duke when he could have any woman in the kingdom?"

She still didn't understand the terror she had now put in my heart, "Don't you understand what you've done to me?" I tried to scream, but my voice broke as I cried.

Mother stood by my chair, then gently placed her hand on my shoulder, "I'm sorry that I lied to you." She let out a deep sigh, "Somehow I was just hoping that things would be different for you."

"And how exactly was it supposed to be different, Mother?" The tears kept flowing down my face, "That when I was a little girl, all of the other children wouldn't make fun of me? Even the milkmaid's boy thought he was better than me because I was so ugly!" I shook my head, so angry and the tears flowed all the faster. "I have borne every insult, every scathing or pitying look by any boy, girl, man or woman who ever looked at my face! All of this I did because I knew one day I would find true love like you did. I thought that if even a man like Father could fall in love with you before you winnowed, that I too might have a chance. But it was all a lie!" My voice broke as I shuddered, gasping between my sobs. I collapsed onto the floor and cried all the harder, "I have no hope."

She sat down beside me and attempted to hold me in her arms, but I pulled away. I know she thought she was helping, but instead it just enraged me further when she added, "You have hope. You know all of this would change if you winnowed. You could pick—"

"I WILL NEVER WINNOW!" I wanted to feel the resolve of what I had just screamed, but inside I didn't. Inside the little voice was laughing at me, "Your sister was right!" it hissed in my head. "No. No. No." I mumbled to myself as I held my hands over my ears trying to block the voice out.

For several minutes, Mother just let me cry. Then she slowly put her arms around me, and I finally let her, my head falling onto her shoulder.

"I don't mean to be cruel, Olive, but you must take the blade with you," she softly said. "There is so much at stake."

"I couldn't live without my powers. The animals are my only true friends. How could I give them up?" I looked into her eyes at last. "It would destroy me."

"I will not ask you to winnow. I will only ask that you take the blade with you. There is a great deal at stake – the peace of this entire country, the life of your father...though I'm sure that means less to you now." She lifted my chin and looked so solemn, "You must promise me that you will do what you must if that is the price that is asked. It is the only blade that will transform you. Any other blade will merely rob you of your powers and you will remain as you are forever."

I didn't want to listen to her words, but I knew there was truth in what she said. Then I realized that if I had the blade, Father would never again be able to blackmail me into submission with threats of removing my crux. Of course I should own the blade! In fact, when I realized how foolish I was behaving, I had to stop my lips from forming into a smile – how stupid I had been.

I finally met my mother's eyes, "I know you are right." I earnestly replied, trying my best to sound contrite.

She slowly hung the blade around my neck. It felt so heavy, this small, powerful blade. I could almost *feel* its evilness as it rested against my skin, but I knew I had my freedom as well. No one would take my powers from me. I would control my destiny at last, even if I now knew I would always be alone.

I watched Lord Rupert from the window as he nervously paced the courtyard, attempting to keep an eye on all of the riches that composed a Princess's dowry. There were chests filled with exotic and precious valuables: luxurious fabrics, spices from the east, a separate trunk of gold coins and jewels. As much as I had asked Mother to fill the treasure chests with rocks and fill, she insisted on the real thing in case I was captured. It galled me that she had so little faith in me, but I would show her I was up to this task.

Mother came in, still looking rather apprehensive, "If you're ready?"

I adjusted the veil around my face, "Yes, I am ready." I wore my grandmother's green dress and held a matching silk scarf in my hand to hide my crux, just in case anyone paid attention. Not many remembered the ways of the Winnowwood, but I would be cautious anyway. I had to succeed, more to prove to my mother that I could, rather than actually saving my father. I suppose that seems cold, but that's honestly how I felt. I was so angry at him. I had always forgiven him almost anything because I thought he had loved my mother as she was, but now that I knew it was all a lie, I just couldn't bear to think of him.

Mother walked me to my carriage, and gave me a long hug goodbye, "Be careful, my darling. Don't let them hurt you. Don't let *him* hurt you."

I knew she was trying to be wise, to give me counsel, "There is nothing he could say that I have not heard many times before." I knew what I would face out in the world,

"What words would I ever expect from a man except a cruel remark. I will be fine."

She hugged me harder, "Yes, you have far more courage than I ever possessed. Please forgive me," she whispered, her voice breaking.

"I'll see you soon," I hugged her back, "With Father." It was hard to look at her face, the face that had betrayed me to my core, but of course I loved her. It was her great shame the lie she had told my sister and me — the truth she wanted to be real, an excuse for her cowardice. That would not happen to me, I swore to myself as I stepped into the carriage.

7

The Highwayman

I watched as the castle faded into the distance. With each second that passed, relief rushed through me. I was finally free from Father. Free from his threats. Free from his scorn. Free from my nightmares. No matter that I was also on my way to free him, he would never have power over me again.

My hand went to the blade that hung from my neck and I clutched it, instead of terror, I now felt power. I would control my destiny and he would no longer have anything to say about it.   A giggle escaped my lips, I felt fabulous.

We had travelled for hours and the sun was now low in the western sky. I'd spent the journey contemplating my future and thought how much had changed since the morning. The reality of my mother's words rang in my head, "... only beauty is worshipped." Well, I didn't want to be worshipped in the slightest, so that was no burden for me to bear, yet, I would still need a mate. Why did the need to find out what was in that potion to drug unsuspecting men keep running through my head? Was I really that desperate? Maybe not today...but what else could possibly be in my future except tricking a man into mating with me? How pathetic.

A wheat field stood on both sides of the road, the tall stalks still in the windless day. I noticed a slight movement to my right, as the wheat bobbed ever so gently. Probably a few deer were hidden in the chest high stalks enjoying their dinner.

Suddenly, the field was filled with over a hundred armed men on both sides of the road – their skin and clothes were colored just like the wheat field and so perfectly camouflaged that I blinked my eyes, thinking them apparitions which couldn't be real. But the voice that shouted was real.

"Black Bart is upon you! Lay down your weapons and your lives shall be spared!" The voice roared, "NOW!" The coach lurched to a halt.

Black Bart? Victore had said he was heartless and cruel and usually didn't leave any witnesses. What could I do to help? My mind raced through options: A Grizzly Bear? A Lion? Could I save my soldiers? Perhaps the best thing to do was fly away and then hunt them down with the Bestiallas.

I stood and hit my head hard against the roof of the carriage. *Stupid. Stupid.* I thought to myself. I couldn't stand and lift my arms over my head as the spell required.

I glanced out the window, a large oak tree stood to the side of the carriage at the edge of the field. I spotted a curious squirrel who watched from a branch. I lifted my veil and called out to him, "It is I, Princess Olive. Help me!" I could tell he heard my voice. He looked at me and gave a curt nod.

"Get her out of here! Quickly! Take the others prisoner. We shall leave no clues as to her disappearance," the voice rang out again. It didn't sound like Black Bart's voice, but I knew I had heard it before as well.

Just then, the door to my carriage was thrown open. A man camouflaged like the rest jumped in, then gallantly tipped his hat. The carriage took off in a rush that threw him down onto the seat. He recovered his balance, then gave me what he obviously thought was a charming smile.

"Good Day, Princess," he spoke as if this was some routine meeting, then immediately pulled the curtains shut on the windows.

As the carriage moved under the oak tree, I heard the smallest of thumps on the roof; my little squirrel had joined us. It made me feel a bit better to know I had one ally on board.

I looked at the man through my veil and studied his face. The intricacies of the camouflage paint were rather remarkable in its detail: at least five different shades of gold, yellow and brown painted in an intricate pattern. Still, I was sure he was one of the men that had been in the grove with Bart when they knocked Rupert off of his horse.

"It is far from a good day, sir. Who are you?" I thought it best to remain civil for now.

"Excuse me, M'lady," he replied in his smooth baritone. "How very crass of me. I am Fabian de Champs of Lordilly, though lately, I am no longer of Lordilly. In fact, I have not seen that part of the world in some time, unfortunately. Though I hope to return at some point, visit the old manse so to speak. Perhaps next year, but then it's been such a busy season…"

What a windbag and what gall, to act like we were at some normal social event. I grew tired of his monologue and interrupted, "What do you want with me, sir?"

Fabian feigned such subservience, "Oh, me? Why nothing, M'lady, nothing at all."

"Then kindly stop this carriage so that I may depart," I shot back at him.

"Oh, no, Princess. I may want nothing from you, but my friend does. You see, he believes you should meet."

He looked so very amused with himself as he spoke that it troubled me. "What friend?" I asked. I was praying that he was not taking me to the infamous Black Bart.

I think he was trying not to smirk, "He's quite well known. Quite the reputation as it were. Though I couldn't be sure you would have heard of him, but then — "

"Who is this friend?" I interrupted, growing more irritated with each second.

Fabian made me wait for it, then smiled as he finally spoke the words, "Black Bart."

It was a good thing he couldn't see my face hidden under my veil because he would have seen my fear. I could feel my heart sink as my stomach did a flip. If what Victore said about him was true, I was in real trouble. I tried to remain calm, not to let my voice betray me, "Black Bart, the Highwayman?"

"Indeed, you do know of him!" Fabian slapped his hand against his thigh with delight. "He will be pleased his reputation has preceded him. He's always quite pleased when—"

My hands clutched my scarf nervously, "What does he want with me?" I demanded.

Fabian grinned all the broader, "I don't mean to speak for him, but if I were a thinking man, I believe your dowry trunks hold a bit of appeal to him."

I let out a sigh of relief, though I don't think Fabian noticed. He was too busy detailing his love of robbing dowry trunks and all of the loot that it would provide for him and his friends. My mind raced. What if everything Victore had said about him was true? I breathed deeply, trying to calm myself.

And then it hit me — what an idiot I was for not realizing it sooner — this is what Bart had done to Rupert when they had knocked him off his horse. They had to have changed the letter from the King or at least read it and resealed it. They knew I would begin my journey today and they had planned to steal the dowry. Mother should have listened to me and filled the chests with rocks!

He has no idea who he is dealing with. I thought of my grandmother and stroked the material of her dress, reminding myself of the power she had wielded. The power I now wield. If only I knew her secrets. I convinced myself that this was a wonderful opportunity. I would see his hideout, unmask his secrets and escape. And then I would lead my father's men there and capture him. We could use the gold.

We had travelled for about thirty minutes when I felt the carriage's movement slow. It bumped and heaved as it left the road then entered a rough riverbed, I could hear the water as it splashed against the wheels. My hand went to the curtains, but Fabian put his hand up to stop mine.

"Please, Princess, you must not look out. The location of Black Bart's hideout must not be made known, even to you, M'lady."

There was a momentary silence, then Fabian went back to regaling me with his exploits in the world of the highwayman, "Bart is rather a seeker of material possessions, you know, enjoys the finer things in life: gold, diamonds, fine works of art. Lately, he's begun to collect paintings, though I don't agree with him on that. I think we need to be more mobile. Don't you? Bandits should be a bit on the cash and carry side of things. Though I suppose he can just roll them up and leave the frames behind, but then, that would seem a bit wasteful, don't you think? No, I much prefer gold...."

I had thought of telling him to be quiet to end his constant prattling, but I'd hoped he might reveal something useful about my enemy, perhaps learn of a weakness, or something I could use against him. Instead, I had endured this soliloquy about the wonders of robbing and looting and only learned that they were very good at what they did.

The carriage lurched again and moved uphill. The sound of the water ended and in a moment, it felt like we were on a smooth road.

Fabian grinned at me, "I think you will enjoy your stay here, Princess. We keep quite busy. What with planning our raids, terrorizing the countryside, counting our booty, indeed, every day is a day filled with a great deal of rather profitable activity, I dare say."

I was ready for them. I knew what I had to do and I knew I could do it. It filled my spirit and strengthened my spine, "I assure you, sir, Black Bart will rue the day he kidnapped me." For just a moment, it was enough to shut him up. The carriage stopped. A few moments later, the door opened.

I recognized the one they had called Puntalo as he leaned in and offered me his hand, "Please step out, Princess. Black Bart awaits you." I stood and took his hand.

Fabian doffed his hat, "I shall look forward to our next chat, Princess. I'm always ready for a bit of clever repartee'."

"I would say, sir, that you truly prefer monologues." I stepped out of the carriage as Puntalo let out a snicker.

I looked around and saw that I was in an immense cave. It was enormous and could easily house over five hundred men. Scores of torches lit the sides of the cave illuminating a vast multitude of armor, swords, cross-bows, helmets and supplies heaped into various piles — all the commodities needed for war. I whispered to myself, "An army out of nowhere." So this is how he'd done it; Black Bart must be in cahoots with the King of Alganoun! It was the only explanation for how my father was captured so quickly.

"Please follow me, Princess." Puntalo beckoned to me.

This highwayman was as powerful as Victore had claimed. Perhaps Victore was right about everything and I was the fool. A shudder went down my spine. I turned for a moment to look back at the carriage. There sat the squirrel staring down at me. "Go for help." I whispered to him. He nodded.

Puntalo turned, "Did you say something, Princess?"

I cleared my throat then let out a small cough, "No." I turned to follow Puntalo to meet my enemy.

As I trailed Puntalo through a maze of corridors and pathways, winding this way and that through the rock, I was astonished with the vast extent of the cave. Who knew this existed? This Black Bart was definitely a rather clever fellow.

I remembered his face. It hadn't seemed so very treacherous that day, but perhaps that was because he had been with his friends. Could he really be as mean and terrible as Victore's stories detailed?

I will not be afraid! I kept thinking to myself as I trudged along behind Puntalo. *I will not be afraid.* I rubbed my hand on my dress. *Watch over me, Grandmother. Show me what to do.* Deep breath. Calm down. *Think of how powerful you are.*

Then Puntalo stopped in front of a door, gave it a sharp rap and waited. After a few moments, I heard his voice.

"Enter," he commanded.

Puntalo opened the door for me as he announced, "Sir, the Princess of Rosemount."

I held my head high and walked in with as much self-assurance as I could command. There he stood, close to the fireplace on the right, the man I had seen in the forest that day, but there was something different about him today that I couldn't quite put my finger on. I walked to the left side of the room to be as far away from him as possible.

"Thank you, Puntalo. That will be all for now," he replied in a voice that commanded assurance.

I could hear him move and he was now a few feet behind me, but I waited before I turned around. I needed a moment to gather my wits.

I looked about the elegantly appointed room, you could hardly tell it was in a cave. Candles cast a lovely light against the walls. At the side of the room was a table elegantly set with a meal for two. Was this for me, or rather, Roseline? Did he think he could impress her with this? I smiled to myself, this was a foolish man after all, if he thought this would have kept my sister from clawing his eyes out given the chance. And then I turned and looked at him and his eyes betrayed him — that was it — he looked nervous!

I watched as he smoothed back the remaining strands of his thinning hair and attempted a slight bow, "Princess, it is so very good to meet you. I am Black Bart."

I was gaining my true confidence back with every second, "Why am I here, sir?" I moved across the room from him to make him keep his distance.

He gave me a winsome smile, "Why, I wanted to thank you for your dowry, of course. I like to give a personal touch to things if I'm not able to attend the event myself."

"That property is meant for a Prince." I decreed.

Bart smugly replied, "Well, if I ever meet him, I shall thank him for it personally. May I see what he has won?" He stepped quickly towards me, his hand moved towards my veil.

I slapped it away, "You may not! I am a Princess. Keep your hands to yourself, sir."

"That was not a request." And with that, he snatched the veil from my face.

I was ready for it. I knew what he would think before he did.

His face registered his shock. Oh, yes, he had planned to steal Roseline. I held my head high and moved away from him. "Close your mouth, sir, it appears you are a frog hunting for flies."

His mouth snapped shut. After a few moments he finally spoke, "Forgive me. It's just... the...uhh, reputation of Princess Roseline is, uhh..."

"Yes, my sister is a great beauty. I, however, am Princess Olive." I declared.

"I didn't know there was a sister," he sighed, then glanced over at his romantic dinner for two.

I smiled at him, what a fool this highwayman was, just another typical male enamored with beautiful women. This would be easy. "Yes, no one mentions me, for I am the Ugly Princess."

Bart turned back to me and attempted to look me in the eye, "You are...are not —" he clumsily began before I cut him off.

"I do not need the lies of a highwayman!"

"I only wanted to say—"

I shoved my face closer to his, "I know what I am! Do you think you could hurt me? You are beneath me!" I said with contempt.

That seemed to anger him, "Hurt you?" He took a dagger from its sheath.

I did not move, perhaps I had misread his actions.

He ran the dagger along my neck, stopping at my jugular vein and placed the tip just so. "Oh, I could hurt you, Princess. If I so desired."

I looked him in the eye, stone cold, though my heart thumped so loudly I was afraid he would hear it and give me away, "But I doubt that would serve your purpose."

He slowly smiled, then sheathed his dagger, "Luckily, it appears what you may lack in beauty, you make for with spirit."

I looked him up and down just as he had me earlier, my nerve returning, "And you, sir, are a fine one to speak to me of beauty."

He seemed rather amused with that remark, "True. At least in that regard, we seem to be on equal footing."

"Except I am a Princess and you are a loathsome highwayman." I shot back at him. I had obviously disrupted his plans. Perhaps he would reconsider, "You will return me, sir."

He now had a look of amusement on this face, "*You* do not order *me*." His voice mocked me with every syllable.

"I am a Princess, you will—"

"I won't. You may be a Princess, but you are now my prisoner."

"For the moment." I stared at him. *If he only knew.*

"No. For a fortnight."

"Unacceptable, sir. I must leave immediately. They'll kill my father if I don't go."

That seemed to pique his interest, "Why? What is it about you that will keep them from killing your father?"

"Because..." I certainly couldn't tell him the truth, that I was going to rescue Father from his prison. He knew what the scroll had said, "...I must marry the Prince of Alganoun as part of a peace treaty." I said it rather matter-of-factly and turned to look at his reaction: he looked amazed. Too amazed.

"You! You are the one to marry the Prince?" he erupted into great hee-haws of laughter.

I couldn't control myself. My hand shot back and I slapped his face as hard as I was able. I think he was as surprised as I was.

He stopped laughing and drew in a quick breath. I could tell he was thinking about his reaction and I was thinking about how quickly I could put my arms in the air and change if I needed to. Much to my relief, he changed his tactic.

"I do apologize for my rudeness, Princess, but for now, I must insist you stay and enjoy my hospitality." He smirked at me, mocking me with his politeness. "I hope that I have your word that you will not attempt to escape while you are here visiting."

I contemplated his request, but my word was my word, even to a scummy highwayman, "And if I refuse to give it?"

He moved closer to me, his anger rising to the surface, "Madam, I have earned my reputation as Black Bart with the Dark Heart. If you would like a demonstration, I will gladly give it."

He grabbed my left arm. He dared to touch me! "Then sir, do your best to contain me as I shall not give my word to an insolent highwayman!" I jerked my arm away and in the process, let loose of the scarf in my hand.

I bent down to pick it up, as did Bart. He reached it first and as he handed it back to me, I felt his gaze upon my left hand. "Then you shall be treated as a prisoner." He looked into my eyes, our heads close together as we knelt.

I slowly smiled, then stood and looked down at him for a moment. "Prisoner."

He stood and looked me in the eye, "Prisoner."

There was something in how he looked back at me that I can only describe as amusement, almost as if my behavior delighted him in some manner. "Puntalo," he barked. Puntalo appeared from the darkness of the hall. "Show the Princess to her quarters. Keep a guard on the door."

Puntalo took a long look at me, completely confused, "Princess Roseline?"

"No, Princess Olive." He said it with such bitterness that it made me react. I looked at him with all of the contempt and derision I could display and then I gave him a slight smile of triumph – he had no idea who he was dealing with.

He gazed back at me with almost a look of confusion. I smiled all the more. How I had ruined his plan. He had no idea how I would ruin him. "Move man!" he ordered Puntalo.

I was only too glad to get away from this highwayman so I could plan my escape. I would enjoy stealing my dowry back from him and everything else he had as well. He would soon be my prisoner.

Once again, I followed Puntalo through the labyrinth of corridors weaving this way and that through the cave. I assessed my situation. Obviously, I could escape, but would that truly be the wisest option? It was clear that this highwayman had helped the King of Alganoun to kidnap my father. He now held my dowry, added insult. No, I needed to find out more about him and this maze of corridors and pathways would help me. It would be easy to hide and to spy and I was so very good at both.

~

The door slammed shut. I turned to examine my prison cell, a rather luxurious room that was set to impress, even a lovely arrangement of lilies on the armoire. An eye for detail, indeed, Black Bart had that, all for my beautiful little sister. I hoped he felt like the fool he was and the fool I would soon capture in turn. He had looked at me with such disappointment. If he only *knew* what he really had, but his eyes blinded him to the truth. Good for me, bad for him.

I moved quickly to the heavy oak door and examined it – perfect. There was a half-inch gap at the bottom. I smiled as I raised my arms over my head, "Anhelo Eximo Muris Winnowwood!" I felt my body fall into itself, drop to the floor and become a mouse. I looked at my left paw and saw the tiny nub sticking out from my pad, Black Bart had not understood what he had seen when he spied my crux. I smiled at the thought of it and headed for the door. *Plenty of room*, I pushed myself under the door and looked about.

The guard was sprawled on a stool, head back against the wall, settling in for a nap. Good. I decided to go to the right and took off down the darkened hallway. I ran quickly, but being a mouse was so slow. I looked about, no one around, stood up on my hind legs with paws over my head, "Anhelo Eximo Cattus Winnowwood!" Now as a cat, I streaked along the darkened hallways and explored the cave. Just as I rounded a corner, I came face to face with a plump, grey mouse.

The mouse froze in fear, she knew I could snap her up and eat her in an instant. "Don't worry, Mouse, it is I, Princess Olive." I took a careful step back to give her a little space.

Mouse was unconvinced and nervously squeaked, "Princess Olive? Here?" Her eyes darted back and forth, searching for a way to escape as she backed away from me.

I took a step closer, and tried to reassure her, "Truly, it is me."

But her eyes were still filled with fear, "Please then, come no closer, Princess. I am but a little mouse."

"I'll show you. Don't be afraid." I stood on my hind legs, my paws over my head, "Anhelo Eximo Muris Winnowwood!" and changed back into a mouse. I smiled at Mouse, whose little face was a mask of shock. "Truly, don't be afraid." I moved closer to her, and placed my small pad upon hers. "Nothing bad will happen to you, my friend."

Mouse looked at my left front paw and spied the little crux sticking out. That seemed to convince her at last. She even managed a little curtsy when she finally spoke, "Please forgive me, dear Princess. It's just so startling to be in your presence. An honor, of course, but so very unexpected."

"There's no need for apologies. I've never visited these parts before." I smiled at her and she returned it, "I would ask you for your assistance, however, if you are willing."

"Of course," she squeaked cheerily.

"I need to find Black Bart. I have concerns he may be in cahoots with my father's enemies and I need to spy on him a bit to ensure I'm right."

Mouse nodded happily, "Oh, I know this cave well. He's probably in the Great Hall. Just follow me." She turned to go.

"It would be faster if I were a cat and you rode me. Would you mind?"

Mouse's eyes grew large, "I think I should like riding a cat," she giggled.

"Excellent!" I stood up, "Anhelo Eximo Cattus Winnowwood," and changed back into a cat.

Mouse looked at me and took a little gulp, but then smiled bravely. I knelt down and she ran up to my head. "Hold on to my whiskers." She gave a little jump, landing lightly on my head, then gently clasped onto my whiskers. I took off at a fast trot. "Are you alright?"

Mouse laughed, "Oh, this is glorious, Princess." We came to an intersection of paths, "To the left, Princess." As we became accustomed to each other, Mouse gently pulled on my whiskers like a bridle and guided me through the long corridors of the cave occasionally letting out a quiet giggle as she did. We made good time. Before long, she softly spoke, "Slow down, Princess, it's just ahead on the right."

I clung to the shadows and sidled up next to the wall. I heard voices. I crept silently forward, slowly rounded the doorway until I could see into the room. My breath stopped. I stopped. There, next to Black Bart, stood a Druzazzi warrior.

Mouse crept close to my ear and whispered, "Move. Under the table where it's dark." She gave my whiskers a sharp tug that jarred me back into reality. I slunk quickly into the darkness under the table and collapsed onto the floor, my head resting on my paws as I stared in shock at them. I hated to think that Victore was right about Bart after all.

From here, I had a perfect view. I took a long look at the Druzazzi and shuddered. He stood towering over Bart, his face painted red, his white hair spiked, clad in warrior's dress with an iron breastplate adorned with a fire-breathing dragon. His hands, however, were bound behind his back in heavy, iron manacles.

To the side stood the same three men I had seen with him in the forest: Puntalo, Fabian the windbag, and the last was the tall one, whose name I did not know. All were armed and were keeping a close eye on the Druzazzi.

Bart appeared completely unintimidated by his fearsome presence and they seemed to be in an argument of some kind. Bart gazed up at the Druzazzi with almost a look of delight, like a cat toying with a mouse. "You think we do not know of your plans? That you've formed a pact with Prince Victore?"

The warrior stared down at him and remained silent. That didn't seem to bother Bart in the slightest. He let out a laugh filled with self-satisfaction, "I have many mercenaries under my employ, Queet. You think my spies have not kept me well informed of Victore's plans? How he convinced King Michael to attack King Ivan?"

If this highwayman was to be believed, I was right about Victore. But was he right or was he just making up a story for his own benefit?

Bart's tone remained confident, mocking, "I know it all, my fearsome friend. You've promised Victore that he will be King of Alganoun and Rosemount if only he will help you with your invasion." For a moment, Queet looked concerned.

I was having a hard time processing all of the information. Bart shouted, startling me further. "But he is a FOOL!" Bart squeezed his fist shut and slammed it on the table for emphasis. He looked at Queet, whose face betrayed a momentary confusion.

"Don't know no Victore," Queet slowly replied.

Bart rolled his eyes, "I thought we were past the lying stage, Queet. Look, I know you need help to land your forces. But you've picked the wrong man. You need *me*. And luckily for you, I am for hire, as are all of my men. See what your money can buy..." he extended his open palm to Queet. On it were two gold signet rings. "...perfect copies of the royal seals of King Michael and King Ivan, depending on who you need to mislead at the moment." He closed his fist, "If you need help with your invasion, you should hire me."

Queet seemed to consider this for a moment. "You cannot be trusted."

Seeing those signet rings answered the last piece of my puzzle — how Bart was able to open the scroll from my father and replace the seal. How in the world was he able to make copies of those rings? More proof that he was working for the King of Alganoun.

Bart smiled brightly at Queet, "Actually, if you check with my customers, you would find they are quite satisfied with my services, but I supposed now is not a good time for comparison shopping."

"You cannot be trusted!" Queet uttered a bit more emphatically.

Bart remained calm, "Fine. Trust Victore. He's a natural born idiot and you will die shortly at the hand of King Ivan." Bart turned his back to Queet and looked at his men, "Geraldo, blindfold this fool then drop him in the forest. Let him find his own way home."

The tall one, named Geraldo, moved immediately to Queet's side, grabbing him roughly by his bound hands and jerking him out of the room.

Bart turned to Puntalo, "Follow him. We must find out exactly where the Druzazzi plan to land. We may not have much time."

Puntalo nodded, then turned to go. "Puntalo." Bart said with concern. He stopped and turned back to Bart. "Be careful. These Druzazzi are butchers. Track him at a distance."

"Don't worry, Bart. I'll be fine." He gave Bart a slight smile of encouragement, then disappeared down the darkened hallway.

Mouse crept forward on my head, "What's a Druzazzi?"

"Evil Incarnate," I whispered.

"Evil in what?" she asked.

I let out a long sigh, "They are bad. They are very, very bad." I didn't know what to think, what to believe. Queet denied knowing Victore, yet, Bart claimed he was part of the plot. And Bart, who I had thought was working for King Ivan, was offering his service in hopes of joining the Druzazzi invasion. It made no sense. Who was the villain? Perhaps, Bart was lying about Victore, but what if he was telling the truth? I didn't know what to believe.

I listened as Bart spoke in a quiet voice to Fabian. "We must find Victore and force his immediate surrender." I wanted to hear him more clearly, so I crept out from under the table and moved closer to the fireplace where Bart stood with Fabian.

"Why bother?" Fabian replied, "The Druzazzi will kill him for us. Victore has always been a bit slow on the intellectual aspects of —"

Bart cut him off, "Yes. Victore is a moron. No news there, but letting the Druzazzi get a foothold back..."

I had made it to the end of the table. I turned and came face to face with a Great Dane, who had been hidden from my view. He looked as surprised as I was, then let out a booming, "BARK!"

"Run!" Mouse shouted in my ear.

And I did. I streaked for the door and escaped before the dog had the chance to react. The last thing I heard was Black Bart hissing, "Winnowwood!" So, he finally figured it out. I suppose seeing a mouse riding an orange cat probably tipped him off at last. I ran all the faster.

Mouse guided me expertly through the maze of corridors. She had quickly become an excellent jockey. "Just a little farther, Princess. We're almost to the entrance."

Behind me, I heard the pounding of footsteps. He'd never catch me.

"I'm so sorry I didn't warn you about that big dog. I should have known he'd be there." Mouse apologized.

"No worries, my little friend. I think I might have been dinner by the time I explained who I was." We turned a corner and there in front of us was the enormous cavern leading to the entrance.

Unfortunately, it was also crowded with well over a hundred men, apparently preparing for movement. "Hold on tight. This may get a bit dicey." I felt her paws hold tighter to my whiskers and her back toes clasp tighter into my fur. I decided the straight path would be the most effective and ran full tilt ahead.

No one was paying much attention to me. After all, it's just an orange cat running...with a mouse on its head! They were all too busy with their preparations to pay me much heed. Good. I was half-way to the entrance, less than fifty-yards away, when Bart's voice rang out behind me.

"STOP THAT CAT!" he shouted.

Luckily, their initial reaction was one of confusion and I continued to streak for the entrance as they processed the information. I'm sure if he had shouted, "Kill that Druzazzi!" they would have had their swords out in an instant, but stopping a cat wasn't high up on the usual skill set of soldiers.

"Grab that cat! NOW! NOW! NOW!" he ordered in a ferocious voice. The men finally leapt into action and ran towards me.

"Hold on tight!" I dipped and turned, a hand closing around nothingness as I ran past him. I heard a giggle from Mouse, her little feet clasped tightly to my fur. A set of thrusting hands closed in on us. I jumped hard and they missed.

"Yee-haw!" Mouse cried out.

Two more men dashed at me from opposite directions. I used my claws and ran up the leg of one of them, then leaped over the other. I could hear the men heads crash into each other's — they both fell to the ground.

"Watch out, Princess!" Mouse shrieked.

I barely caught the man diving for me out of the corner of my eye. I dug my claws into the earth and changed direction. Another miss. I dived and dipped, ran through legs, over backs and made it to the cave entrance. I heard the rush of footfalls behind me as they ran after me. They'd never catch me once I made it out of here. Only a few more yards, then daylight at last.

There to greet me were so many of my friends: Bear, Wolf, Cougar and a score of others. That wonderful squirrel had managed to call them for me. I ran to them and took shelter behind Bear.

The men began to pour out of the cave entrance. The animals growled and roared at them. They froze in place as they were unarmed, not thinking they would have need of weapons chasing a little cat after all. Slowly, they backed up into their cave, then turned and ran.

I changed back into myself, Mouse now sat on my head. I took her gently into my hands, "Thank you, my friend. You are such a brave little creature."

"It was so fun, Princess," she beamed back at me.

Just then Black Bart ran out of the cave, then stopped in his tracks when he met my greeting party. Side Stripe stood next to me, his ears flat as he growled at Bart. I placed Mouse on his head, "Please, watch over her for me, Side Stripe."

"Of course, Princess," he looked back at Bart and snarled even more ferociously.

"Well, well. If it isn't the man himself." I smiled triumphantly at Bart, knowing he knew I had heard all that had gone on in his meeting. I must say, his face looked rather ashen.

"Olive, you do not understand what you have heard." He finally sounded desperate.

"Now my ears lie to me, sir? I think not. You were the one who ambushed my father. You want to assist the Druzazzi in invading our country!" I shouted at him with all of the anger and fear that I felt.

He looked at me with absolute earnestness, or at least as earnest as a highwayman could be, "Believe me, Olive, you are dead wrong. We captured him and I was *lying* to him! I just wanted to get him to tell me of their plans."

"Ah, the words of a highwayman. You think me a simpleton, sir." I turned to the animals, "We must leave, they will quickly be upon us. Head back to the glen." I quickly changed into an eagle and took flight.

I gazed downward and saw the men rush back out of the cave, now armed to the teeth. Too late. I could see Bart shading his eyes as he watched me. I dipped a wing and waved goodbye at him. I had won this first skirmish with him, but feared what would happen the next time I encountered him.

A Bluebird flew next to me. I asked, "Do you know where Victore's camp is?"

She nodded, "Yes. He's in the forest close to the sea, north of here."

"Would you guide me there, Bluebird?" She nodded again, then tilted her wing and we headed north. As I flew beside her, I wasn't sure what to do. Was Victore a traitor? Had he betrayed my father or was he the only ally I had left to help me rescue him? I thought of Bart's words when he had spoken to that horrible Druzazzi. Where was the truth? I needed to find that out. I had to know what part Victore played in this before I could decide my own course of action.

We had flown quickly for twenty minutes over the high hills that protected the coastline. Bluebird looked over to me, "There, Princess. Just over the rise, next to the river."

"Yes, I see it." Victore's camp came into view. It was less than a mile from the sea, not far from where I had followed him that day. I soared over his camp, he had to have well over four hundred men with him from the number of tents I counted. What was he doing here? If I listened to Bart's words, I knew what he was doing — waiting for his white-haired friends to show up.

"Are you going down there, Princess?" Bluebird asked.

"Yes. I have to find out what he's up to." She shot me a look of warning. "I'll be careful," I assured her.

"I shall keep flying overhead and keep an eye out for you then."

"Thank you, my friend." And with that, I dove down to the camp to look for Victore. I found his red banners around the largest tent, it had to be his command tent. I looked for a place where I could land unnoticed. There, a small grove of trees by a fallen log. It would provide the shelter I needed. I quickly alighted and changed back into myself. I lay on the ground behind the fallen log and had an excellent view of Victore's tent.

Everything seemed quiet. I wondered if he was even in the camp. Then I saw the soldier outside Victore's tent entrance snap to attention as the door flap was pulled open and Victore emerged. He was wearing his armor and grinning like an imbecile. I had seen that look on his face many times before, smug and self-satisfied. It made me want to smack him. I bet that would surprise him and wipe a bit of that smugness away.

But a moment later, when a Druzazzi warrior followed him out of the tent, smacking Victore was the last thing on my mind. I felt the blood drain from my face, my hands suddenly cold as a chill ran down my spine. Bart had not lied, Victore was the traitor! God help us.

How he had promised my father his loyalty as he had goaded him into launching the attack on King Ivan. How he had baited him and manipulated him into doing exactly as he desired. Never mind how he had manipulated Roseline as well. We now stood on the edge of the cliff of doom and Victore would help to push us into oblivion. I needed to escape. I needed to find my friends then plan a way to fight them.

As I turned to stand, a Druzazzi was standing right behind me! Before I could raise my arms, he back-handed me with such force, I collapsed into blackness.

8

Victore

Pain coursed through my body, my head pounded where he'd hit me. I felt the ropes that tied my hands to a chair as well as the gag that had been placed across my mouth. I couldn't move. I was living my nightmare. Panic filled me to the bone. The sound of voices arguing finally drifted into my mind and pierced my consciousness.

I recognized that voice: Victore. I opened my eyes just a fraction of a slit to see where I was. Across the room, Victore argued with two Druzazzi. The one I had seen talking to Bart at his hideout that he had called Queet. The second one just looked like a squatter and smaller version of him.

Victore seemed highly irritated, "How can you believe a highwayman?" he snapped at them.

Queet eyed him suspiciously in return, "He knew we join forces. Knew you betray King Michael. Maybe knows we land tomorrow on Fandollini Spit on the tide!"

"You cannot believe those lies!" Victore shouted. "I have not betrayed you. I have no idea how this highwayman has figured this out!"

Queet moved in, attempting to intimidate, "Black Bart seems to know you. Said you pay him."

"And he is a LIAR! I do not know this ridiculous highwayman."

"How can he know of plan?" Queet questioned him in a quieter, more menacing voice.

"Have you ever thought that perhaps he was bluffing? That he was fishing for information? That he had no idea you were involved, that is, until they captured you in the forest for God's sake!" Victore roared with just a hint of hysteria in his voice. He knew he was on the knife's edge and this man could kill him before his guards could stop him. He looked accusingly back at Queet.

Queet was dangerously calm, "Killed spy sent to follow me. I not stupid."

Poor Puntalo, I thought to myself. He seemed a rather decent sort. Just then, I noticed a small movement under the flap of the tent to the left. Mouse crept in. She looked up, our eyes met and she gave me a little nod and disappeared back under the tent.

"The only one who does know when you are landing is this ugly beast of a woman." Victore's voice snarled with disgust as he rushed over to my chair. I closed my eyes and let my head fall forward. He grabbed my hair and snapped my head back, "Oh, stop faking it, Olive. You think I didn't notice those beady eyes peering about?"

I tried to speak, but the gag prevented that, so I lowered my head and wouldn't look at him.

Victore put his face close to mine, he sounded so smug and pleased with himself. "Oh, want to say something? Like your little charm for turning into some creature?" He let out a mean snicker, then pulled my hair harder forcing me to look at him, "Roseline told me how your magical powers work. That's why I've tied your arms down and gagged you," he hissed.

He stood back up and smiled, "Gather round, gentlemen, for she is the last of them. The last of the Winnowwood!"

That got the short one's attention, "Legend is true?" he asked in disbelief.

Victore grinned happily, "Indeed it is."

His eyes were on my neck and the golden chain that held the blade that was tucked into my bodice. *Oh no, don't see it. Don't see it*, I prayed to myself.

His hand shot out and in a split second, he grabbed the Blade of the Winnowwood from around my neck. "Olive, I can't believe you have this on you! Roseline said you swore never to use it," he exclaimed with joy. He turned to the

Druzazzi, "With this little knife, she will turn into the most beautiful woman you've ever seen."

The short one scrutinized me closely, "Seen better looking dogs," he decreed.

Queet added his insult, "Not possible. Too ugly."

"Ugly?" Victore restated, "Man, she is an abomination! But, if you would like to watch the last conversion of the Winnowwood, all we need to do is take this blade and cut off..." Victore grabbed my left hand, "...this blighted branch on her finger under the moonlight and she will become a real beauty."

Queet liked the idea of violence mixed with beauty, "Would like to see that." His nasty tongue flicked around his lips like a thirsty dog. "Huh, Surty?" He glanced at his comrade.

"Yes, cut off finger." Surty agreed.

Victore saw he had them fully back on his side. "Either of you need a wife?" He leered at them, and then made this laughing, horrific gargle of a noise. "Help me move her. Keep her bound and gagged. Don't want her turning into some sort of animal on us."

I tried to scream, "No!", but it just came out as a garbled, muffled choking noise. I couldn't believe this had happened. I had escaped my father and finally felt free, yet, this buffoon would be the one to take my powers from me. This idiot: Victore.

I was the idiot. My sister has accused me of arrogance before, and now, I guess she was right. I had underestimated him and would now pay for it with my life. The only life I wanted. My life was nothing without my powers. The little voice was silent in my head. What no, "I told you so." No, "This will be good for you." Even the little voice realized it was best to shut up right now.

Victore clasped the chair on my left, "Get the other side."

Queet grabbed the other side and they lifted me into the air. I felt the tears stream from my eyes and run down my cheeks. *Oh you foolish, girl, why did you come here alone?*

Just then, the bright light of the moon cast a silhouette of a large cat passing by the tent, a loud snarl followed it. I felt the chair fall, then slam into the ground; my head missed a large rock by inches.

Queet had dropped his side and unsheathed his sword in a split second, "Look!"

Surty glanced frantically about, "Where's spear?" then grabbed it and ran to the door.

My friends had come to rescue me! My heart soared, but as I watched Surty run from the tent, I was terrified my friends would be hurt. Loud howls erupted as four huge wolves ran past the tent.

Victore turned to me bewildered, "How did you call them here?" A slow moving growl followed a large bear as he lumbered past. "Sound the Alarm!" Victore cried out, then he leaned over and snarled at me, "I will kill them all, Olive. Do not think you safe!" He smiled as he hung the Blade of the Winnowwood around his neck, "I'll keep this for now." Then he turned and ran out of the tent.

I tried to free my hands, but they were still tied tight. I could hear the shouting of voices from outside, "Over there!

Kill it! Get it!" How many of my friends would die trying to save me? *Why hadn't I listened to Bart?* He had been right about everything.

The sound of ripping behind me. Something was coming into the tent, but I couldn't move to see who it was. Someone to kill me or someone to help me?

In a moment, there was Bart cutting the ropes from my hands, removing the gag from my mouth, "Quickly, Princess." He took my hand and helped me to my feet, then pulled me to the back of the tent that now possessed a five-foot rip for our escape.

"YOU!" We turned. There was Queet. He recognized Bart and threw his dagger — it was headed directly for me!

In a flash of movement, Bart thrust his body in front of mine, protecting me in his arms. He let out a gasp of pain as the dagger struck him deep in his left shoulder, then grabbed my hand and pulled me out of the tent. "Run Olive, save yourself!" he cried out to me.

I pulled the dagger out of his back, then grabbed his right hand and put it over my shoulder, "Just hang onto me!" I stretched my arms over my head, "Anhelo Eximo Equus Winnowwood!" and in an instant felt my body expand as Bart gripped onto me and I changed into a horse. I shouted, "Run, my friends! I am free! Run to the glen!"

I heard Bear take up my roar, "To the glen! Princess Olive is free!"

The Birds joined in the announcement, "She is free! She is free! Run! Run!" The birds dive-bombed the Druzazzi and Victore's men and spooked some of their horses with their caws and shrieks as their claws and beaks assaulted the soldiers.

I ran quickly and tried to keep an eye on everyone else as we made our escape. Suddenly, a Druzazzi soldier leapt from the bushes with a spear aimed at me. As he moved his arm to throw, Side Stipe jumped up and closed his jaws on the soldier's hand and held on. Mouse dangled from his ear, her little paws clutched tightly to his fur.

The Druzazzi pulled a knife and before I could stop him, stabbed Side Stripe, who let out a terrible whimper, then fell to the ground in a heap. I kicked the soldier in the head and he fell down unconscious. "Bart, please get that little fox."

Bart slid down my back to the ground and hobbled to the motionless Side Stripe. Mouse still sat on his head. Bart carefully picked them up and held them close.

I knelt down to make it easier for Bart to remount, then we were off again. I rushed onward, but could hear the sound of the pounding hooves of the enemy's horses behind me. I turned my head and spotted the mass of soldiers who followed a scant thirty-yards behind. I looked to the birds flying with us, "Tell those horses to stop chasing us!"

The birds took off. A few moments passed and I could hear their shouts to the horses behind us, "Princess Olive orders you to stop chasing us!" I heard the horses stop dead in their tracks, then the sound of riders flying forward unimpeded to the ground. A handful of horses ignored their orders and galloped onward – it seemed they all had Druzazzi on their backs, perhaps they didn't understand. I'd have to get rid of them as well.

Grandmother, please help me, I prayed before I shouted, "Anhelo Eximo Fulgar Winnowwood!" Nothing happened. I shouted out again, "Anhelo Eximo Fulgar Winnowwood!" I looked into the sky with disappointment. *Why couldn't I make a lightning bolt?* I knew my grandmother had been able to do it. How I wish I knew how to harness my powers!

I changed my chant, "Anhelo Eximo Pluvia Winnowwood!" At last, something worked — rain began to fall from the sky. I shouted it again, "Anhelo Eximo Pluvia Winnowwood!" The sky opened up in a torrent of rain that washed away our tracks and provided us our escape. We changed direction and headed for the glen.

9

The Glen

~

Thirty minutes later, we were there: our refuge. The glen was still dry as I had ended the rainstorm a mile previously when we had turned up the hidden pathway that led to it. Bart slid off of me, cradling Side Stripe in his arms as he stumbled to the ground. He could barely stand, his wet shirt stained with his own blood and Side Stripe's.

I stood tall, towering over him, and would have laughed at the stunned look on his face, but I was too worried about Side Stripe. I turned back into myself and quickly took Side

Stripe from him then sat down next to the fire pit. I listened to his chest.

Bart collapsed onto the ground next to me exhausted, "I'm sorry, Olive, but I think he may be dead," he sadly stated, Mouse peeked down from his shoulder.

I picked up the faintest of heartbeats, "No. Not yet. Hold on, Side Stripe. Hold on." I quietly begged him. I placed my hands over his wound and began my chant, "Anhelo Eximo Sano, Salus, Sanu. Anhelo Eximo Sano, Salus, Sanu." My hands began to glow. I felt it spread to my face, through my body until even each of the hairs on my head luminesced with the bright, green light. I was beginning to find Side Stripe's spirit, but it was difficult, he was so far away. Finally, I felt him in my mind, becoming part of me. I chanted with even more fervor and felt the soldier stab us with his dagger. I felt my teeth release the soldier's hand and fall to the ground. *What a brave soul Side Stripe is*, I thought as my spirit began to heal him. I felt our strength return and finally finished my chant.

I opened my eyes as the green luminescence quickly faded from Side Stripe's body and mine. All of the animals had gathered closely around us, worried for their friend.

I looked over to Bart who stared at me, his mouth agape. I suppose it was quite a sight to watch me turn into this bright green healing spirit. He probably thought I was a hideous freak. I glanced away. *Stop it, you are powerful and fearsome and could not care less what a stupid highwayman thinks of you.* But I knew he wasn't stupid, after all, he rescued me as much as

I rescued him. I took a deep breath and looked back up at him.

Bart really didn't look disconcerted about it in the slightest. He slowly looked away and eyed all of the animals who would obviously protect me if he tried anything. Bart shifted his gaze back to me, he had an odd look on his face, then he smiled. If anything, it looked more like he was in awe of me than repulsed. That felt strange.

"That was amazing," he quietly stated, "Truly, amazing."

Side Stripe's eyes opened and he softly nuzzled my hands. I gently stroked him, filled with relief, "Rest, my dear Side Stripe." I placed him carefully by the fire pit, then touched the wood and it leapt into a blazing fire.

"Nice trick," quipped Bart.

I felt my cheeks grow hot, and tilted my head down so that my hair would mask my face. "Now, let me have a look at you." I knelt next to him and began to remove his shirt.

"It's not too bad. Please, don't trouble yourself," he stated casually.

I examined the wound — Queet's dagger had pierced him rather deeply, at least three to four inches and he would need stitches. "I'd hate to think what bad is if this isn't. You've lost quite a bit of blood. I need to get my supplies." I rose quickly and went to the storage shed and retrieved bandages, needle, thread, blanket and a pan for water, which I filled from the lake. Bart looked tired when I returned.

I opened the blanket on the ground next to the fire pit. "Please lay on your stomach."

Bart moved to the blanket, letting out a low moan as he did. He rested his head on his right forearm, tilting his head back to watch me. Perhaps he was wary I wouldn't sew him up correctly.

Mouse seemed to have grown fond of Bart and continued to sit on his shoulder as I tended to him. I began to clean the dried blood away from the gash. "I'm sorry to tell you that my powers have no effect on humans, just the rest of nature." I rinsed the cloth, "My sister and I used to try it on each other, the servants, Greatpapa and any other willing subject when we were small without any success. I'm afraid I have nothing more than water, herbs, bandages and a needle and thread."

"I think you lie to me, Olive," he said quietly.

"Unlike you, I do not lie."

"You just do not wish to heal me. Why would you?" his voice waivered as he grew weaker.

"True. Help the man that kidnapped me? That would have seemed far-fetched if you had asked me this morning."

His head turned towards me, "It has been a rather odd day."

"You were certainly the last person I thought would rescue me," I said softly.

"Glad I could surprise you," he tried to smile.

I looked at him through my tangled mess of hair, "Why did you save me from Victore?"

He took a slow, deep breath, "You misunderstood what you'd overheard and I knew you'd be walking into a trap."

"How did you know that?"

"My men captured Queet on a patrol. I was attempting to trick him into telling me when and where the ships were landing. Given what you had heard, I knew you would think me the villain," he said almost guiltily. Then he continued his confession, "You see I am actually in the employ of King Ivan of Alganoun."

"Yes, I figured that one out for myself when I arrived in that cave and saw all that it contained — an army out of nowhere. That's how you so easily captured my father."

"King Ivan is a good man," he said solemnly.

"As is my father." I caught the laughter in his eyes, "He is my father, I can do without the sarcasm." I could tell from his expression that he thought my father as big of a dim-wit as I did.

"I didn't say a word," he added, feigning innocence.

He didn't need to, I could hear the laughter in his voice, "Your eyes, sir..."

"And your eyes are beautiful, Princess," he smiled at me in the most disarming of manners.

I felt the blush begin again and dipped my head away from him. This man was a conundrum to me. I had never heard a kind word from a man in my life, except Greatpapa and he was a relative. Bart had been such a posturing dolt when I had first met him in the cave, yet now, he almost seemed nice. It was all so confusing, "Try not to pull the stitches out." I focused on finishing the last stitch and cut the thread. "Now, please sit up."

He slowly pushed himself up. I began to wrap the bandage around his chest to secure it. It was so strange for me to be this close to a man, a half-dressed man at that. Yet, here we were, alone in the middle of the forest at night, except for all of my animal friends who lurked closely by my side. They rarely spoke when there were humans around. "Please lift your right arm. Hopefully, that doesn't hurt."

"No, that arm is fine," he smirked at me with a half-smile.

He had such a nice smile. Again, I could feel the blush begin and worked to secure the bandage. "I admit my father was a fool to listen to Victore." I felt his eyes on me and dipped my head down, so my face was hidden in the chaos of my hair.

"Victore is assisting the Druzazzi with the invasion of our lands. They have promised to make him ruler of both of our kingdoms," Bart solemnly stated.

"The Druzazzi will kill him." I could tell from my short experience with Queet and Surty in the tent that they were not to be trusted.

"Yes. Then they will cleanse the land of the lot of us if we don't stop them," he let out a long sigh. "Victore's folly has brought our most feared enemy back to our land while we are at our most vulnerable." He moved his head, trying to get a better look at me.

I shifted away from him and pushed my hair in front of my face, "Yes, we are vulnerable." I felt far too vulnerable at this moment.

"I did not believe there were any true Winnowwoods left." He placed his right arm under his head to prop it up, Mouse still sat on his shoulder.

I glanced over at him, "I believe I am the last."

He was smiling at me, "I must admit when I saw this little mouse riding you out of the room — it was a sight indeed." Again, he looked at me as if he admired my actions, "How did you make it rain?"

I looked away in embarrassment, thinking back to what I had tried to do and failed. "I was trying to do so much more than that."

"But it looks like you just speak words and it happens."

"It's more difficult than just speaking, rather hard to explain." I paused and he waited for me to find my words. "It's like it has to come from within me, from my heart or something or nothing happens."

"Within you?" Bart looked puzzled.

"It was supposed to be thunderbolts and lightning and I made it drizzle."

"That was far more than a drizzle, my Lady."

"It was not what I had wanted. I couldn't do what I wanted." I said with frustration.

"But you healed Side Strip so easily."

"For some reason, that's always been easy for me. It's just when I try something big, like lightning that…" I shook my head in sadness, "…I guess I really don't understand my powers, yet, I am the only one left."

Bart looked at me, "I'm sure you'll find out their secret."

I could tell he wasn't teasing me, and that he truly meant it. It made me happy that he believed in me. "I hope you're right." I looked back over to him, "You know we killed most of the witches with lightning bolts."

"That must have been some trick. I would have loved to have seen that," he laughed, his eyes began to close with exhaustion.

"You need to rest." I wrapped the blanket about him. "Go to sleep, Bart."

His eyes opened for a moment, the pan of water next to him, reflecting my face, "There is a beautiful woman in the water." He whispered as he stared into the pan.

I ran my hand through the water to disrupt the reflection, "Just an illusion. Rest now."

His eyes closed. I watched the even fall of his chest as he fell into slumber. What a strange man this was. What a strange day. I sat close to the fire and reflected on all that had happened.

Black Bart actually worked for King Ivan and had captured my father. But now I could see that was just a step in Victore's plan. He had lured Father into attacking King Ivan knowing he would be captured, taking him and our men off of the field of battle so he could assist the Druzazzi with the invasion of our country. It was rather diabolical and had more brilliance to it than I would ever have given Victore credit for conceiving.

And now, what could we do? Tomorrow they would land on the tide and the situation appeared completely hopeless. I looked around at my friends, at Bart, and knew we would all die. I felt the tears come and tried to blink them away. At least I could warn them. I went to the shed and found paper and ink and wrote out a message, then looked for my best messenger. "Owl?"

"Hooo-ooot," he replied from the tree, then fluttered down to a lower branch.

"Would you take this message to my father held prison in the middle turret of Alganoun Castle?"

"For yo-oou, I do-oo," he hooted back at me. I held the rolled message up to him and he clasped it tightly in his talons.

"Please hurry, then return and tell me what happened when he read it."

He nodded, then took off into the night sky lit by the full moon. I wondered if my father would believe me. He'd better. I walked slowly back to where Bart lay sleeping on the blanket.

"I like him," Bear said softly. "He is brave." Bear was staring at Bart as he rested his head on his paws, a thoughtful look on his enormous face.

"Yes. He is an unusual man." I moved over next to Bear, sat down and rested my head against him. "Thank you for coming to my rescue — twice today. I guess my plan was a poor one."

"Not at all. You just did not realize the immensity of what you were up against," he consoled me.

I let out a small gasp as reality hit me. *Tomorrow. We would probably all die tomorrow.* I clutched my hands into Bear's fur, "What will we do? I don't know how we can defeat them." I felt the hot tears cascade down my cheeks. "I don't know if we'll be able to save our people."

Bear slowly sat up and positioned himself directly in front of me. His liquid brown eyes reflected the flames of the fire, "You will save your people," he solemnly stated.

I wiped the tears from my eyes, "I've seen these butchers in action, Bear. They are ruthless!" I stared into his eyes, the reflection of the flames mesmerizing.

His face became more emotional as he stared back at me, "You are Olive, Last of the Winnowwood! You can rain fire on them if you choose!"

I couldn't stop myself, I began to cry all the harder, "But I don't know how to do it, Bear! Didn't you watch me fail tonight? I tried to make a lightning bolt. I tried with all my might! I couldn't do it."

He placed his huge paw on my shoulder, "You will find a way to do this."

"But I don't know how. I've never known how! Everyone will die because I don't know how to use my powers," I choked the words out, barely able to speak.

"You have the power. I know when the time comes, you will save us all," he calmly stated, then moved his paw and laid back down and continued to stare at Bart.

I laid my head against Bear's shoulder and closed my eyes. I was exhausted. And terrified. I tried to think of what I had done wrong, but all I could think of was my grandmother and wished so much that she was here to help me. I fell asleep.

I woke up startled by my own screams. Terrible images of Druzazzi warriors killing my people, my family and my friends still clear in my mind. The one they called Queet had been about to cut off my crux. I let out a long sigh of relief as I came to my senses, putting the dream out of my reality, at least for now. My hand subconsciously reached for the blade that had been around my neck, then I remembered Victore had taken it. I looked up.

Bart was staring at me, "Are you alright, Olive?"

I didn't want to tell him that I knew we were doomed, that I was weak and stupid and foolish, that no one could rely on me to save them because I was an ignorant idiot! "Just a bad dream." I pulled myself to a sitting position, "I should ask you the same."

Bart slowly sat up as well, wincing slightly as he did. He slowly extended his left arm, "It will be difficult to swing a sword for a while. Good thing I'm even better with a bow."

"My, but you are a highwayman of many talents." I stood and moved over to Bart to check his bandage. I sat down next to him and inspected the wound, my stitches had held.

He gave me a crooked smile, "As are you, lady. Many talents indeed." His face turned to a look of concern, "What is that on your face? Did they strike you?"

I pushed my hair around my face and dropped my head, "No. Well, yes. A Druzazzi soldier did hit me, but…" I moved away, closer to the fire.

Bart edged closer to me, "Please, let me see. Perhaps you need some attention to your injury."

"No, I'm fine. Really." I scooted farther away from him.

Bart stopped, "What is it?"

"I thought you knew the Legend of the Winnowwood?" I quietly asked.

"Yes, I do," he confidently replied, "All women. They can turn into animals. They're known for their beauty..." Bart immediately realized his mistake and attempted an awkward retraction, "...I mean, not all, I'm sure, but..." He mumbled to a stop, embarrassed by his own insensitivity.

I don't know why I wanted to tell him, to punish him for his gaff or to actually talk to him. "You are wrong about the Winnowwood being a beautiful people. In truth, we are quite ill-favored."

"But your mother, I have heard, as I have heard of your sister, is quite, uh, lovely," he stated awkwardly.

"They weren't born that way. They were born with the gift that you have seen me use today." I moved my head toward the fire to keep him from seeing, "Beauty is not a gift we are born with, it's one that was given to us by a witch to curse our kind."

Bart's face showed his confusion, "Cursed you? But then, how are they...uh, so lovely? That doesn't seem like much of a curse."

I took a deep breath and continued, still wondering why it now seemed important to tell this highwayman the truth. "You would if you understood what they traded. You see, we have a choice."

"A choice?" he looked over to me, obviously confused.

"There is a small knife called the Blade of the Winnowwood, and if you use it to cut off this..." I held out my left hand with my branched finger, "...you become very beautiful."

"But then, why are you..."

He was trying to find the right word, so I helped him, "Ugly?" I looked over to Bart, "Well, you see there is a price to pay. You lose all of your magical powers. You are then only a mortal. A very beautiful mortal."

Bart was considering what I had said, "That is indeed a high price to pay."

"I am surprised you think it such. All men have demanded it of the Winnowwood Women..." I could hear the sharp edge in my voice, "...just as my father did of my mother before he would marry her."

Bart shook his head in apparent disbelief, "I'm sorry to say it, as he is your father, but he is a natural born idiot! After what I saw today? Amazing! How could anyone choose to give that up?"

I was surprised at his response, obviously he still didn't truly understand. "Well, you see it becomes more difficult as one grows older. Every time I use my powers, I become uglier." I paused for a moment, "Needless to say, after what I did tonight, I am quite a sight. That's why you see me as I am."

Bart still stared at me, "But I can't see you, Olive." I still kept my head down, my hair obscuring any view he might have. "As I mentioned earlier, Olive, in that regard, we are equals. You have nothing to fear from me regarding appearances."

"Is that why your mouth fell open in such disappointment when you pulled my veil from my face?" I shot back at him.

Bart frowned, "I am sorry. Small children have been known to run at the sight of me." He paused, "I know how it feels to be judged from your appearance instead of what is in your head, what is in your heart."

For some reason, this struck a nerve with me and the words rushed out of me, "But it isn't the only thing you're judged on. I mean, you are still notorious: Black Bart with the Dark Heart, not homely Bart with the ugly nose." I looked down, feeling defeated, "I shall never be known as anything but the Ugly Princess." I glanced over at him.

His hand went to his nose, feeling its bridge, "You don't like my nose?"

"Oh, I'm so sorry. I didn't mean it like that—"

Bart interrupted me with a laugh, "I'm joking, Olive! See, you are lucky. You know you could become beautiful whenever you choose it." He smiled at me, "But I will stay as I am, and might I add, with no magical powers."

I could feel myself smiling in return, "Perhaps you will consider me less fortunate if you know that you and I are now the same, for my choice is gone and my future only holds more warts, lumps and bumps." I ran my hand gently along my face, seeking out the new damage that was assuredly there. "I must say, I feel rather strange knowing there is no longer a choice. Not that I would have taken it. It just, hmm, I don't know." It was odd admitting this. I would never have used the blade, yet, not having it around my neck, I now found rather unsettling in itself.

"What has happened to take this choice from you?" he asked.

"Victore took the blade from me." I tried to make light of it, "If you hadn't come along when you did, all you would have found was a beautiful woman tied to a chair."

"Thank my lucky stars that you hadn't changed or Queet would have had me skinned by now."

He smiled at me again. I could feel myself smiling in return, "I think that short, squat one was looking for a bride."

"We're both lucky then." He moved slightly closer to me.

"Yes, we're very lucky," I whispered. I didn't move. I could feel him shift closer to me as I gazed into the fire. I decided to see what he was made of and turned my face towards him in the light of the fire, knowing that he would now see me clearly.

Bart's face showed no shock, no change in manner as he gazed upon my face, "It's not so bad, really, a few new warts, and a small bump. After what you did, I expected Medusa."

I felt the tears start, yet again, so I turned my head to brush them away. What was I turning into? A big crybaby? But this was so surprising, that he would be so kind. It was overwhelming. "You're a kind man, Black Bart. Best not to let your enemies know."

"Are you my enemy?" he asked in a soft voice.

I slowly looked back to him and smiled my reply, then turned back to the fire. This was a very strange man. Could he mean what he said? Could he truly be this kind? This was not the man Victore had described. In fact, when I thought about it, Victore had been describing himself: vicious, disloyal, and heartless.

I still felt his eyes on me. I know it seems insane but for some reason at that moment, the thought crossed my mind that just maybe I wouldn't have to use a magical potion on Bart for him to mate with me. The shame of that thought made my face flush. How could I think like this? He was a highwayman for heaven's sake!

I was glad that Owl decided to return just then and noisily announced his arrival as he landed in the tree overhead. "Ne-eeeew information for you, Princess."

"What has happened, Owl?"

"All at Alganoun now run about like crazed ants. Screaming. Shrieking. They are preparing."

"Thank heavens, Father listened to what I had written," I let out a sigh of relief.

"He tried to sho-ooo me away, but finally read it." Owl stated, "He is a foo-ool," he gently hooted.

"I know," I agreed with a sigh.

"What have you done?" asked Bart.

I looked at him and began to truly trust him at last, "The Druzazzi are arriving tomorrow on the tide," I calmly stated.

Bart's mouth fell open, "What?"

"Yes, they were speaking of it in the tent when Victore captured me." I looked over to him, "You almost convinced them that Victore was the traitor...almost."

Bart shook his head taking in the information, "There is much to do."

I paused for a moment, knowing the news I had to tell him next would hurt him, "I'm sorry to tell you this, but I also heard Queet say that he had killed Puntalo."

Bart's face fell with sadness, he looked away to the fire for several moments.

"I've sent word via Owl to my father who has told King Ivan. All of Alganoun is making preparations."

"I must go," Bart stated determinedly, but as he tried to stand, he leaned too far on one of his legs and stumbled back to his knees.

I moved quickly over to him and offered him my hand to help him up. "You are in no position to go. You are wounded, you have no horse and you are my prisoner," I teased him.

He took my hand, then slowly stood, standing close to me, "Am I?" he asked as he looked into my eyes.

And for a moment, I stared back at him. He smiled his crooked smile and his eyes teased me with something I had no experience with – was he flirting with me? Oh, I could feel my cheeks begin to burn and hoped the dim light of the fire didn't expose me, but I didn't look away. I couldn't help but smile back, "Just until the dawn, which will be here shortly. I like the idea that I held Black Bart prisoner..." A giggle escaped my lips! Was I turning into Roseline? I stopped the giggles immediately, "...for a bit longer than he held me."

"Clever girl. I've been a prisoner to no man and now I am prisoner to a woman."

I had convinced Bart to go back to sleep for a few hours, then I returned to lay on Bear's shoulder and watched him

sleep. So many thoughts raced through my head, our immi-
nent annihilation should have been foremost, but for some
reason I only thought of his smile. His eyes. His kindness.
This was a completely new experience for me. I had been
very good at protecting myself from the scorn of men, allow-
ing myself rarely to think of it, never dwelling on it, but now
I stared at Bart.

His face was peaceful, it made him look gentle, certainly
not the vicious highwayman described by Victore, but then
Victore was a big fat liar and nothing he had said could be
trusted. How foolish I had been in underestimating his cor-
rupt nature. I had completely miscalculated his viciousness.
I let out a sigh and cursed my own foolish arrogance. How
I thought I had Victore all figured out, yet, if not for Bart's
actions, chances are I would now be Victore's beautiful prisoner — powerless and probably given to the Druzazzi to do as
they would with me. I shiver ran down my spine as I thought
of that future.

Bart had saved my friends as well from a fight that would
certainly have been costly in life. Bear would have fought to
the death for me as would the others. I stroked Bear's fur,
knowing that he was still at risk, that we were all at risk, but
at least we had made it safely through this day.

I stared back at Bart and let my thankfulness for this man
wash over me. As I watched him, the last thing I remembered before I fell back to sleep was the way he had smiled
at me.

10

A Lesson In Killing

The day had dawned dismal and foggy with a chill in the air. I inspected Bart's bandage again – the wound had closed nicely. Given what I knew was on the horizon for this day, I wrapped it with extra padding and ensured it was tight and secure. I felt his eyes on me. I was feeling brave, so I let my eyes meet his.

He had a strange look on his face as we gazed at each other, it was almost wistful. After a few moments, he looked up at the sky, "This fog will hide them from our lookouts on the coastline."

I wondered what he really had been thinking because it was not the fog that would create that expression. "Let me enlist some help." I stood and walked over to the trees, "Dear birds, would you please help me?"

A Robin, a Crow and a Raven fluttered to the rocks next to me, "Yes, Princess," said Raven.

"The Druzazzi fleet is to arrive on the tide near Fandollini Spit. Could you please find the Seagulls and ask them to fly out over the sea and find their ships for us as quickly as possible. It's terribly important."

"Of course," announced Crow. They immediately took to the sky with a multitude of other birds joining them.

Bart looked amused, "Well, I have no idea what you said, but it certainly appears efficient."

"Hopefully." I answered, then turned to my friends. "I'm sorry to ask this of you, but I must beg you to gather all the animals of the forest and meet us in the woods by Fandollini Spit. I will meet you there with soldiers as well. It will take all of us to save our world today."

Bear stepped forward, "You are the High Priestess of the Bestiallas. We are *yours* to command." He lowered his head in a sign of respect to me, as did all of the other animals.

I formally curtsied in response, "I thank you. And I pray that by this night, we will be safe from these barbarians at last."

I looked over at Bart. His face was filled with respect as he met my gaze, then he formally bowed as well. I prayed I wouldn't let them all down, but that seemed impossible.

❧

I ran through the forest with Bart on my back. With every step, I grew more and more fearful. In my heart, I hoped that the outcome would not depend on me. That my father's and King Ivan's men would be enough to repel the invasion. That there would not be too many ships. That I would not have to face them alone. But my heart told me that my hopes were not to be. Inside, I knew that all of my fears would be realized if I could not harness my powers.

I stumbled on a root and nearly fell over. Bart gripped my mane and neck tightly in peril of falling off. "I'm so sorry," I stopped to allow him to regain his seat.

Bart repositioned himself, his knees now tight against my sides, "I'm fine. Go ahead."

I began to run again, this time I focused on where I was going. "Olive, I can feel your anxiety," Bart gently stated. I didn't answer him, just kept on running. "You were at the battle the last time?" he asked.

"Yes." That was all that had been running through my mind: the memories of those ruthless barbarians.

"I remember seeing you that night and thinking that you were such a brave little girl."

"You aren't that much older than me."

"True. I was sixteen then. You were what, twelve?" he asked.

"Eleven. Did you fight?"

"Yes. I was one of those who climbed the cliff and shot them from above."

"Ah, you're even better with a bow — you said that last night. I think I watched you in action. I was flying over the battle that night." I paused as I thought of all that I had seen, "So much death." My breath broke and I gasped in a long drink of air.

"Would you allow me to give you some advice, Olive?"

"Why not." I dully replied, still I suppose a highwayman might have some insight into battle strategy.

"When the battle starts, don't think of them," he solemnly stated.

I nearly snorted out a laugh, his advice seemed so ridiculous, "That seems a foolish thought. If I don't think of *them*, what would you have me think of?" I said sarcastically.

"Think of all the people, all of the animals, that you love. If you think of them, you will not be afraid. Their love will make you strong. If you think of the Druzazzi and their terror, it will fill you with fear and you will not be able to think clearly," he calmly stated.

I contemplated his words. "That seems a bit easier said than done," I replied. "As I recall from that night, it seemed that the fear I felt was highly motivating."

"Yes, terror can be motivating, but that is not where your power lies. I am a good commander in battle because my mind is clear. My mind is clear because I am not fearful. I am not fearful because I know why I am there — to protect the people I love."

"Again, I think easier said than done."

"Perhaps." Bart paused for several moments before he went on, "I don't enjoy killing." Again, he hesitated before he continued, he was quite solemn when he spoke. "I do believe the Druzazzi truly enjoy the killing. They're raised on the blood and worship death. Their training is brutal and many of their own die by their hand in mere training exercises. At that last battle, when I would look into their eyes, there was this crazy rage that I can't define. It was merciless, wanton, maleficent. I knew that kind of rage did not exist in me, and initially, it terrified me that they would win because of this rage, of this infernal desire to kill. To me, it was almost like an entirely new weapon was in their possession and I did not have it. I think I almost hyperventilated to tell you the truth."

"I doubt that," I interjected. When I had watched Bart with that Druzazzi Queet, it was like he was speaking to some regular person he worked with.

"No, truly, I did. My breathing became erratic and I knew I had to calm down if I had a chance at surviving the battle. And so I thought of my father, my sisters, my friends and it began to calm me. It seemed to calm my aim as well and I began to pick them off one by one. I would just say, "For you Father. For you Sister, for you Uncle and on and on all through the night. I went on like that for hours and I never repeated the same name. The more people I named, the surer my aim became and the surer my will was that I was doing the right thing."

"How many did you kill?"

After ten seconds or so, he finally answered, "That night I killed two hundred and eighty-seven of our enemy."

I mulled over what he had said and found it puzzling, "You have a lot of family and friends for a highwayman."

"I'm a people-person, what can I say?"

I could hear the laughter in his voice and could almost see the lop-sided smile that would be on his face. "I'll try to take your advice, but I can't promise anything."

"I'll hope you find it helpful. I don't deny the fear, Olive. Just the way through it is the path I have found."

I continued to run and didn't reply, but in my mind I knew I had added a person to my list: Bart.

As we neared Bart's hideout, I remembered that my original plan had been to bring my father's men here to arrest Bart and that was how I anticipated my second visit to his cave would occur. Yet, here I was carrying Bart back myself and I now felt he was my only hope in defeating our mortal enemy. He had saved me from Victore and had proven himself kinder than any man I had ever met. It would seem all of my previous thinking had been faulty, and it left me feeling rather out of sorts.

When we arrived at the entrance to the cave, Fabian was walking out. When he spied Bart on my back, his assault began, "Where have you been? We received word from King Ivan that the Druzazzi are invading on the tide only hours ago. The Druzazzi! How they are coming, I have not a clue to how this happened."

Bart held up his hand, "Yes, I know. Are the men prepared?" he calmly asked and dismounted.

I stood tall, my hooves high in the air over my head. Fabian's mouth fell open as he stared, moving back, wary of me. "Winnowwood Equus Eximo Anhelo!" I cried out and returned to my human form. Fabian still stared at me dumbstruck, not replying to Bart's question.

I smiled at him, then heard Bart let out a chuckle as well. I couldn't resist, "Good Day, Fabian," I said casually. He only continued to stare at me. "Indeed, this is quite a day when you have nothing to say." I grinned at him.

Bart offered his arm to me, "Princess." I took it and Bart escorted me into the cave.

After a few moments, Fabian finally snapped out of it and followed us at a run, "Yes. Yes! The men are ready. The men are ready!"

11

Tricked

An hour later, we had left the cave with all of Bart's three hundred and fifty-five men, armed to the teeth. I rode one of Bart's horses, but she had not minded. She said it was an honor to carry me and when she looked at me, I could tell that she believed in me too. I wish I felt her confidence.

We had travelled for several hours and it had to be after noon, but I couldn't tell. The thick fog still clung to the lowlands and it was impossible to see the sun through it. As we approached the line of headlands and bluffs that guarded the coastline, the eerie, fog-filled landscape made me feel like I had lived it in some previous nightmare.

Bart and I were in front, leading the long column of men up the North Road to Fandollini Spit. Occasionally, I would hear a few snickers drifting up from the men. I was used to snickers when I did not wear a veil. Bart would just look over at me and give me a bit of a smile, a nod of encouragement.

It made me set my jaw. Made me sit up a little taller in the saddle. Reminded me of who I was and helped me to try to master my fear, but I was still terrified. *Grandmother, please watch over me today.* I thought to myself. *Please show me the secret to my powers. Please. Please. Please.* I prayed. I was still wearing the same dress — her dress. How could this all have happened in just over a day?

I felt Bart's stare and glanced over at him, "Are King's Ivan men ready?" I tried to sound casual, even though my heart pounded desperately in my chest.

"The rider said they left for Fandollini Spit before the dawn. They should be there by now," Bart replied.

"It could still be a trap. They know I heard everything. They might have been able to change their landing plans at the last moment."

"I'll hold back my men in case they manage it," he said with assurance.

But I didn't feel assured. I still had this all-encompassing feeling of woe that I fought with every breath that I took, trying desperately not to let it take possession of me. *Help me be brave, Grandmother. Help me find the secret to my powers. Please, Grandmother.*

I think Bart could sense my panic, I could feel his eyes on me, but we rode on in silence. I felt like such a coward, maybe he thought that as well. That made me sad. I wanted him to think well of me.

Suddenly, the sky was filled with shrieking! Then hundreds of Seagulls broke through the fog, filling the misty air with a white whirlwind of shrieking and furiously flapping wings. I understood their cries, "They're coming! They're coming!" My stomach did a flip flop and I wanted to vomit.

Bart's men were unnerved from the sudden appearance of all of the birds, a few even drew their swords and waved them wildly at the birds. An Old Seagull landed on my shoulder and whispered the words into my ear, "We found them. They are south of the spit. Far south. Ships almost to shore. Just the other side of these hills. Ships almost to shore! Already sent word to Bear. Hurry! Come with us!"

I stroked his head for just a moment, "Thank you, Seagull."

He took off, flying low over the soldiers as he waited for me. I turned to Bart, "It is as we feared. They have changed their plans. They are landing to the south of the spit, just on the other side of these hills.

Bart looked grim, "They would have the high ground." He thought for moment, "We must turnaround. Buckmeade pass is a half mile back. It will get us there quicker."

Our eyes met, we both knew what was at stake. "I'll go ahead. Maybe I can think of a way to delay them."

Bart's face filled with concern, "Be careful, Olive. I'll get there as soon as I can."

I jumped down, took a deep breath, then lifted my arms over my head and cried out, "Anhelo Eximo Aquila Winnowwood!" and changed into my eagle form and flew off. I looked down at Bart, he gave me a quick wave.

I glanced back to those toads that had snickered at me earlier and their mouths were now open in shock. I felt like flying over them and letting it fly, but I had no time for such silly vengeance. Not when we were all about to die.

As I joined the Seagulls that circled above, I looked down and spotted one rider speeding up the North Road. Bart must have sent him to warn King Ivan about the new landing point. I heard Bart cry out, "To the pass!" as he spurred his horse and the procession looped back in on itself and began to run back in the direction of Buckmeade pass. I could only pray he would get there in time.

I flew fast, leaping through the sky, and was over the hills in seconds, bursting through the fog as I rose high in the air. Fog covered all of the land in a thick, white blanket below me except for the top of the bluffs that poked through it like balding giants' heads. I heard them before I saw them. A rumbling death chant echoing out from the mist.

I followed the sound, then dive-bombed back down into the thick, white mist. When I finally popped out of the dense fog, visibility was limited to a hundred yards I would guess, but it was enough for me to find them, to see them. It was a nightmare.

Four immense ships were less than half a mile from shore filled with screaming Druzazzi — faces painted red, white spiked hair, beating their massive swords against their shields as a single drum beat as they as they chanted in unison, "KILL! KILL! DEATH! KILL! KILL! DEATH! BLOOD! BLOOD! DEATH! BLOOD! BLOOD! DEATH!" Yes, they had shields this time. This time, they were prepared. And we weren't.

On the shoreline waited Victore, Queet and Surty with over three hundred of Victore's soldiers carrying red shields the color of blood. There were also about a dozen Druzazzi on horseback behind Queet. It must be the scouting party Bart had discovered.

I flew over the four Druzazzi ships, each held about one hundred men. Looking at Victore's men and the ships, they would have at least seven hundred men. They would out-number Bart over two to one. The little voice in my head just kept whispering, "Death," to me. I shuddered with fear.

I winged towards the shoreline and looked for my friends in the forest. I spied Bear at its edge approximately four hundred meters south of Victore's men.

I turned to the old Seagull, "Please, have your gulls tell those horses to dump those men and gather on the north end of the beach. I will speak to them myself."

"Of course, Princess," the Seagull replied, then shrieked to his flock. "Come on, gulls! Time for some dive bombing!" He plummeted downwards with hundreds of seagulls spiraling behind him. That alone would have been enough to spook the horses as the seagulls converged on them, but then the horses heard their instructions, "Princess Olive warns you! Dump them! Dump them! Catastrophe awaits!

Run! Run to the north! Run to the north! Princess Olive will meet you there!"

The beach erupted with the whinnies of the horses as they bucked and stomped, throwing their riders to the ground. I could hear the thuds of the soldiers falling to the sand in their heavy armor, their surprised cries.

I flew over the beach and spotted Victore falling to the ground as he cursed, "What in blue blazes!?" and landed on his back staring up at me. He would know I was here. I wasn't sure if that was good or bad actually.

I watched the hundreds of horses run to the north side of the beach before I headed to Bear at the edge of the forest. In a few moments, I landed and I changed back into my human form. There before me was a multitude of animals awaiting my orders. I was overwhelmed. There were hundreds of animals who had attended my birthday party, but now there were thousands of animals who stood before me. And I didn't know what to do! I felt like such a fraud.

"Lookey! Lookey!" shouted a small rabbit and a group of field mice as they pointed at the shoreline.

I turned to look and saw the sails come down on the ships, the oars were out as they stroked hard for shore, now, only a hundred yards away. I shuddered, "They're beaching the ships on shore!" I couldn't keep the hysteria from my voice.

Cougar slinked over next to me, her face perplexed, "What does that mean?"

Tears filled my eyes, "It means they aren't leaving." My heart pounded so fast, I was light-headed.

The screams from the ships, as they rowed in synch, filled the air like some deadly aural poison, "KILL! KILL! DEATH! KILL! KILL! DEATH! BLOOD! BLOOD! DEATH! BLOOD! BLOOD! DEATH!"

I was terrified, but knew I had to find a way to stop them. "I've got to try. I've got to try," I mumbled to myself, though I knew I would fail. I raised my arms my arms over my head, "Anhelo Eximo Fulgar Winnowwood!" I shouted. Nothing happened.

I tried to focus. To concentrate. I clenched my fists over my head, "Anhelo Eximo Fulgar Winnowwood!" Barely bursting through the foggy mist above, an insignificant lightning bolt briefly illuminated the sky, then fizzled out without so much as a boom. We were doomed. "I can't do it. I can't do it!" I sobbed in desperation.

Cougar moved forward, "We will kill them for you!"

That shocked me back into reality. I looked out at the ships, the first had already reached shore and its lethal warriors were jumping over the side into the shallow surf and heading to shore. The other three ships were right behind, their evil, murderous crews preparing to disembark.

"No. They could kill you. Some of you would die," I cried.

Wolf looked at me and I could sense his disappointment, he seemed surprised that I was so worthless, "We will do it for you, Princess."

"No. Not yet. Let me think." I rubbed my temples and tried to think clearly. I thought of something I knew I could do, at least it would be a start. "Let's get them distracted."

I raised my arms over my head, "Anhelo Eximo Vespa Morsus Winnowwood! Anhelo Eximo Crabo Ictus Winnowwood!" I screamed with fury, "Anhelo Eximo Vespa Morsus Winnowwood! Anhelo Eximo Crabo Ictus Winnowwood!" And then I heard it – a quiet buzz that grew louder and louder until a roar filled the air.

Suddenly, a dark cloud of hornets and wasps burst through the fog from the forest and rushed towards the soldiers on the beach. The men ran into the water in a desperate attempt to escape the onslaught. Unfortunately for them, they ran smack into the imposing hoard of Druzazzi soldiers wading ashore. The Druzazzi tossed Victore's men aside like they were irritating children, then slapped off the hornets as if they were no more pesky than a mosquito, but after thirty and forty hornets attacked their arms, their eyes, their lips, even they ducked under the water to escape the stings.

More and more hornets and wasps appeared until an immense, dark cloud of them hovered just inches over the water, eagerly attacking any of them that came up for air. I could see the hornets flying down their throats, their noses and the men hacking and barking with pain.

It may just be a swarm of stinging insects, but at least I had figured out a way to keep them in the water for now. It made me feel a little more confident, but how to set up a trap to bring them to us in the forest? A plan began to form in my mind.

I turned to Bear, "That should keep them busy for a while. I'm going to ask the horses to help us. Bear, please get all of our biggest warriors in front. We'll set up a decoy and surprise them."

I changed into an Eagle and flew high over the battlefield then headed for the horses at the north end of the beach. When I looked down at the dark cloud of hornets hovering over the water, I swear I saw Victore look up at me. His face disappeared. I couldn't tell for sure if it was real or if my fear was just getting the best of me.

I knew the soldiers would be desperate to get those horses. If I had the horses run back to the beach towards where Bear and all of the animals waited, they would follow them into the forest and then we could annihilate them! Or so I prayed.

I descended into the midst of the horses and turned into a horse as well. "Hello, my friends."

All of the horses bowed their heads for a moment. A few of the Druzazzi's horses hesitated at first, but as the other horse glared at them, they too bowed their heads, "My Princess."

"There are thousands of animal warriors waiting to tear the invaders apart on the north end of this beach in the forest. I need you to run back to the soldiers and lure them into the woods by letting them chase after you. Do not be afraid of the bears, cougars and wolves that are in the front. You know they will not hurt you. I will protect you all the best I am able."

"As you say, Princess. We will follow your instructions," one of Victore's horses replied. In fact, as I looked at him, he was Victore's horse!

I moved next to him and placed my nose on his, "Thank you." We stared at each other a moment. He simply nodded and bowed again.

I looked over to the immense horses of the Druzazzi, "Will you help as well?'

One of them, an enormous chestnut stallion, stepped forward, "They are hard men and they have used us ill. We will be glad to assist in their death." He too bowed his head.

I slowly looked at them all, then I bowed my head, "I thank you." I glanced back down the beach, the dark cloud of hornets still held the soldiers in abeyance. "Wait for my signal, then run towards the soldiers like you are going to let them mount you. Then, before they can, run into the forest where we will be waiting and we will destroy them."

"It will be as you say," Victore's horse assured me.

"Then I shall see you again soon." I changed back into my Eagle form and took off. I finally felt a bit optimistic, that just maybe this could work. I could heal my friends if they were hurt. I wouldn't need the lightning bolts, which was a good thing since I couldn't create any. We could do this. I looked down at the beachhead.

Happily, the swarm of hornets still had the soldiers pinned down in the water. I was looking ahead trying to spot Bear when it happened. I heard a whoosh of air and before I could react, something hit me. Something hit me in the head and then all the world turned to darkness.

12

To The Death

"Is she dead?" I heard Bear's voice. "I WILL KILL THEM ALL!" he roared.

"I'll rrrrr-rip them apart!" added Wolf.

I felt a soft touch on my chest. "Her heart still beats. I hear it," said Side Stripe. Then I felt his tongue licking my head. I opened my eyes.

The Animals gasped in relief. I slowly stood, shaking my head to clear the pain, then fluffed my wings and lifted them over my head, "Winnowwood Aquila Aximo Anhelo!"

and changed back into my human form. My hand went to my head and I could feel the gash on the side of my temple.

Bear moved close to me, "Are you alright?"

"What happened?" I stood still as I gathered my wits.

Bear's gravelly voice told me the details, "When you flew back, Victore shot you with an arrow. The seagulls broke your fall as you fell to the ground. The hornets left as soon as you lost consciousness. You landed on the beach and Victore was about to kill you, but Cougar ran out and rescued you and brought you back to us."

Cougar had moved next to me as well. I knelt down, "Thank you, my friend." I hugged her as she licked my face, cleaning my wound, then I kissed her nose.

"The battle. What has happened?" I asked.

"Just as Cougar rescued you, Bart's men appeared and they have managed to keep the others in the water," Bear solemnly stated, "but it is not going well."

I ran to the edge of the forest, searching for Bart. I found him, just as an arrow hit his horse. It bucked in pain, and Bart fell to the ground. His horse took off down the beach towards the others who were still waiting for my signal. I'd have to scrap that plan, Bart and his men were in trouble and needed our help now.

The Druzazzi swarmed in from the sea, far out numbering Bart's men. I watched as Queet moved in on Bart, his humongous sword raised for the kill. My blood ran cold, not Bart! I turned to the animals, "We must help them. Prepare for battle!"

Great growls and hisses rose up from the crowd. What should I become, what would help the most? I remembered my favorite book and knew in an instant. I raised my arms over my head and cried out, "Anhelo Aximo Elephantus Winnowwood!" then charged out to the beach.

I rushed forward with my Bestiallas Army. I would save Bart first. I watched as Queet slashed viciously at him as Bart parried the blows, but I knew he was weak, his wound would not allow him to hold his sword for long.

Queet moved in again as he slashed and screamed at Bart, "I kill you like I kill your friend." He knocked Bart to the ground and lifted his sword.

But by then, I was close enough and let my shriek fill the air as I blew through my trunk. Queet's face looked up at me in shock. What, he'd never seen an orange elephant in his life? I suppose he had never seen an Elephant at all. He was still staring up at me when I pounded him into a puddle into the sand with my giant foot. "For Puntalo," I stated. I looked over to Bart, "Are you alright?"

Bart stared open-mouthed at me as well, but managed to give me a nod of encouragement. I guess he had never seen an elephant either.

My pack of carnivores stood with me. I turned to face the line of Druzazzi and soldiers in the water, "CHARGE!"

Over two hundred Bears, Wolves and Cougars were in the front line with me, followed by Horses, Deer, Elk, Moose and Foxes behind them. With shrieks and roars we headed for the onslaught.

And they ran for the sea! The Druzazzi ran for the sea! I was so happy, I nearly shouted with joy. We had them on the run and we followed them. They would not escape us. When I reached the water, I placed my trunk in the surf and cried for the creatures of the sea to help as well.

I looked to the Druzazzi – they were getting long spears from their ships – better for goring and stabbing my friends. Well, I would fix that. I moved to the first ship, standing high in the shallow surf, I brought all of my weight down in a fury upon the side of the ship. The sides shattered into splinters and the ship fell onto its side, water quickly filling the broken hull.

The remaining Druzazzi and Victore's men now slogged through the water back to the other ships that remained, as they sought protection. I was now so glad they had beached their ships – there was no way for them to escape!

To my left, a Druzazzi lifted his arm, spear in hand and aimed it at Bear. From twenty-yards away, I sprayed him fiercely with water from my trunk and he fell over from its force.

Suddenly, one of the soldiers disappeared under the water. Then another. "Sharks!" one of the soldiers screamed, just as a huge, Great White Shark breached high out of the water, pulling another Druzazzi under the water with him as it submerged.

The terrified men looked at each other, then at the shore with my army of carnivores. Bart's men had gathered behind us, bows at the ready – arrows nocked and ready to fly.

Two more men disappeared under the waves, just as a dozen Great White Sharks breached the water behind them. It was spectacular! That was it.

"WE SURRENDER!" They began to shout as they struggled to the shore, throwing their weapons down. "We surrender," they pleaded.

I turned and moved back out of the water.

Bart stepped quickly to my side, "Let me take it from here." Bart signaled to Geraldo and Fabian, "Take their weapons. Tie them up."

"I haven't found Victore." I spoke, my trunk close to his ear.

He regarded me with an amused look on his face as he stared at my trunk, then looked me in my green elephant eyes, "I'll keep an eye out. The coward's probably hiding in the forest."

I moved farther back with my pack, staying close enough to keep an eye on things in case Bart needed help. Bear sat next to me. "Oh, Bear. We've won." I softly spoke.

His face watched the crowd of Druzazzi being processed by Bart's men. After they turned in their weapons, Bart's men then tied their hands behind their backs. "So it would appear," he finally replied.

Surty now stood in front of Bart, glaring at him with a murderous look on his face, "Best treat us right, Highwayman. We are a vengeful lot."

Bart stared at him for a moment, "You will receive the mercy from us that you would never have given."

Surty slowly enunciated his reply, "We will kill you to the last man. Woman. And child. Until you are no more."

The way he said it made a chill run down my spine. Something *was* wrong. I stood on my hide legs, "Winnowwood Elephantus Aximo Anhelo!" and turned back into my human form.

All of the soldiers were staring at me. I didn't care. *Stare all you want*, I thought to myself. I rushed to Bart's side. "Something is wrong."

Bart looked at me and smiled, "What do you mean? We have won because of you." He took my hand in his and raised it over our heads, "To Princess Olive, who has saved us from our enemy!"

Geraldo shouted out, "Hip! Hip!" Bart's men still seemed to be stunned. Just a few mumbled, "Hooray."

"Come on men. Princess Olive has saved us! Hip! Hip!" Geraldo shouted. Finally, getting over their nerves, the cheers began, "Hooray!"

More men began to call out, "Hooray for Princess Olive!" "MY PRINCESS! MY PRINCESS!" they began to shout. They clapped and yelled, jubilation finally taking over.

I was overwhelmed. I had never been cheered in my life, and now to have hundreds of men shouting my name was rather incredulous. I looked down, letting my hair hide my face, but I couldn't help but smile.

Bart still held my hand and he gave it a squeeze, "You are amazing, Olive."

I looked up and searched his face, I had never been met with such a look of acceptance and admiration. I could feel myself blush. It seemed like the sun was shining on me. And it was. The fog was lifting and I could see the sun at last.

A scream of terror filled the air, "LOOK!"

And we did look. Everyone's eyes turned to the sea as it revealed what the fog had hidden: Over a hundred Druzazzi battleships approached the coast!

13

Deliverance

They were about two miles offshore and would land in minutes. As we all stood there, momentarily stunned, we could hear the chants drift over the water. "Kill! Kill! Death! Kill! Kill! Death! Blood! Blood! Death! Blood! Blood! Death!" muffled by the surf, hinting of what was about to come. My blood turned to ice as the shock of this attack hit me. I stared at Bart, his face was filled with anguish. He held tightly to my hand.

A horrific gargle of laughter broke the silence. It was Surty. He smiled at us, his broken, black teeth formed in a sneer of delight, "Kill, kill, death. Blood, blood, death." He almost whispered the words, making it all the more terrifying. Geraldo struck him in the head with the hilt of his sword. He fell to the ground unconscious.

Bart looked into my eyes, his face filled with defeat, "We won't be able to stop them."

I looked down at his hand in mind and clasped it with both of my hands. I took a deep breath and tried to focus, to remain calm. I looked back into his eyes, "Get everyone off of the beach. Hurry." I tried to turn and pull my hands away, but he still held them tight.

"It is impossible," he solemnly stated.

"No. I will do what I was meant to do."

But before I could move, he took me into his arms and hugged me in an embrace, "Be careful, Olive. Please, be careful," he whispered fervently in my ear.

After a few moments, I pulled back and stared into his eyes, "You be careful as well." I finally pulled my hand away, then turned and ran up the beach to the Bestiallas.

Bart turned to Geraldo and Fabian, "Clear the beach! NOW!" The soldiers and their captives moved out quickly in response to his command.

I ran to Bear, who had organized all of the animals by species and viciousness. "We will kill as many as we can!" he thundered.

"No. I want you to go into the forest, high up on this hill behind the bluff. You will wait for me there." I ran my hand along his cheek as I hoped in my heart that I would see him again.

Bear would not have it, "But Princess, you cannot do this on your own."

I looked him in the eye, "I can make it rain fire if I desire!"

Bear stared into my eyes, "You are Olive, Last of the Winnowwood!" he said with a roar.

A calmness took over me. A calmness I had never known in the face of such danger. "I am Olive. And I will save my people!" my voice resounded over all of the animals. I raised my arms over my head and cried out, "Anhelo Eximo Aquila Winnowwood!"

As I flew above them, I watched the Bestiallas run for the forest and Bart's men clear the beach. It was now empty and only awaited the impending landing of the enemy. I spotted a high bluff and quickly flew to it. I raised my wings over my head and shouted, "Winnowwood Aquila Eximo Anhelo!" and returned to my human form.

I looked out at the sea. The ships filled with the butchers. The shouts of their death threats. Their only desire to kill my people. My people! No – that was not going to happen. I thought of Bart's words to me earlier that morning – think of the people you love and it will clear your mind. It made me smile when I realized I was thinking of him.

I would do this. I would destroy them. I would not let fear take hold of me. Not now. Not ever! I raised my arms over my head and began my chant, "Anhelo Eximo Aquilo Winnowwood!" I called to the wind and felt a slight breeze. *For my people, my friends, my family, **I will do this**!*

"Anhelo Eximo Aquilo Winnowwood!" I cried to the wind a second time. The calmer I was, the more powerful the wind became. I thought of my mother. My sister. My animals. The soldiers who had cheered me. Our people. And Bart. And I began to feel my power!

"ANHELO EXIMO SUPERNA WINNOWWOOD! ANHELO EXIMO NOTOS WINNOWWOOD!" I called to the south wind, then the north wind…and the wind began to intensify.

I could feel everything. I could feel the winds bending to my will – willingly. They wanted to help me. My mind was filled with images of the things I loved: my mother's hug, the soldiers' cheers, the animals' devotion, my birthday crown, the blessing my mother had given me and Bart's smile.

"ANHELO EXIMO PORCELLA WINNOWWOOD! ANHELO EXIMO TEMPESTAS WINNOWWOOD! ANHELO EXIMO SUPERNA WINNOWWOOD! ANHELO EXIMO NOTOS WINNOWWOOD!" My voice boomed with authority and the winds listened.

Dark clouds were forming quickly over my head as I chanted, "ANHELO EXIMO TURBO WINNOWWOOD!" I called to the most powerful wind. I felt sparks shoot out from my fingertips as my body became more and more translucent as the wind intensified and I became the wind.

The sea had turned from dark blue to a roiling, greenish-grey sea of destruction. Giant white capped waves broke over the bows of the Druzazzi ships. They stopped their evil chants and began to look nervous. Thirty-foot waves began to pound the beach, washing up to the edge of the forest.

I smiled with joy as I could feel my power grow, "ANHELO EXIMO TURBO WINNOWWOOD!" I chanted and chanted as I turned in the wind, becoming all the more powerful, all the more translucent.

I was the calm in the eye of the storm. The images of my mother, Bart, the animals, continued in my mind. And then I felt her – my grandmother's spirit! Tears of joy sprang from my eyes for I could see her green spirit standing right next to me. "ANHELO EXIMO TURBO WINNOWWOOD!" She joined me as I chanted. I stared at her and she smiled. My heart exploded with love, she was here to help!

I changed my chant and called to my fallen sisters, "ANHELO EXIMO WINNOWWOOD! ANHELO EXIMO WINNOWWOOD!" Grandmother nodded her approval and suddenly a great green cloud of swirling Winnowwood spirits surrounded me and their voices joined with mine, "ANHELO EXIMO TURBO WINNOWWOOD!" Our voices, now a roaring chorus, commanded the most powerful wind to our will.

Before my eyes, the power of our words became real. The wind pulled the waves into towers of death. The Druzazzi ships now appeared like children's toys in a sea of tidal waves. One by one they overturned and the sea greedily took them to her depths until only one ship was left – the largest ship – the Commander's Ship!

I stopped my chant, my Winnowwood sisters halted as well. Finally, feeling my power to the bottom of my soul, I boomed out," ANHELO EXIMO FULGAR WINNOWWOOD!" An enormous bolt of lightning exploded across the sky, striking the ship and blasting it into nothingness.

I stared at the now empty sea — they were all gone! A laugh escaped my surprised lips. Grandmother laughed as well, then my other sisters joined in. The sky above cleared and the sun shone again and I watched in awe as all of their green spirits rose into the air, then disappeared on the breeze with a last sound of laughter as they went.

"Thank you, Grandmother. Thank you, Sisters!" I tried to shout out, but it was no more than a whisper. I was utterly drained. Tears still flowed from my eyes, both from gratitude and exhaustion. It was over. I had done it. We were safe. We were all safe again!

I heard a sound behind me and turned to look, but before I could, I was thrown to the ground. There above me stood Victore.

14

Lost

~

Victore pinned my arms harshly to my sides with his knees, then he looked at my face and pulled back in horror. He stared at me in shock as his mouth fell open, a look of disgust covered his face. "And I thought you were ugly before," he hissed at me.

I could see it on his face and it dragged me back into reality. I couldn't image what I must look like after all of the spells I had used, but if Victore's face was any indication, it must be very, very bad. The tears start anew, though I don't think I had stopped crying. First, from joy, then from exhaustion, and now from reality. What had I done to myself?

Victore's face went from one of horror to suddenly looking completely delighted with himself. An evil smile filled his wicked face, he pulled out his own dagger and held it to my throat. I could see the Blade of the Winnowwood that still dangled from his neck.

"I was going to kill you, Olive. You have ruined all of my brilliantly calculated plans," he pushed his blade hard against my throat, then he let out a malevolent chortle of laughter. "But I have decided on a much more fitting punishment for you to endure." He grabbed my left hand.

I could see it in his eyes what he planned to do. I tried to fight him, but I was so exhausted, I had no strength left. I tried to call for my grandmother, but not so much as a whisper came out of my voice with the knife pressed so tightly against my throat.

He pulled my hand up to him and held it tight. "Dying is too much a blessing for you, disgusting beast!" He smiled at me, then with a quick flash of motion, cut off my crux with his knife.

I watched as it turned into black dust and dissolved into the air, leaving a black scarred circle on my left little finger. I stared in shock at it, then looked back up to Victore's victorious face.

"No more magic, Olive! You are now trapped in this hideous shell. Everyone who sees you will be filled with revulsion. I have cursed you forever!" he sneered with glee, so delighted with his wickedness.

I imagine he got about five seconds worth of delight before the arrow appeared in his chest and he crumpled to the side — dead. I looked in the direction the arrow had come from and saw Bart on his horse riding quickly up the bluff. Bart! For a moment, my heart soared, then it collapsed back to earth — I didn't want him to see me!

I wiggled out from under Victore's body, and tried to stand. I made it to my feet and my hands made it to my face, and I collapsed to the ground as the shock hit me. My hands could feel the devastation — there had to be more than forty new warts and there was a lump on the left side of my face that felt huge! That was probably the lightning bolt I guessed. I wanted to run away, but my feet refused to comply. Instead, I tucked myself into a tight ball, my hands clenched across my head.

I heard Bart's horse ride onto the bluff then the sound of him jumping to the ground. "Olive!" he ran to my side, "Olive, are you alright?" I didn't move, just clutched my knees to my chest all the harder. I felt Bart's hand touch my left hand where the new black circle was exposed. I heard him gasp in sorrow, "Oh, Olive. I'm so sorry."

I heard him move over to Victore's body and he took something, but I couldn't see what it was between my tears and my face tucked protectively away. Bart was next to me again. He tried to put his arms around me, but I held tighter to my head and tucked harder and smaller into a ball. "Leave me, Bart. Please. Leave me." I pleaded.

I felt Bart's arms around me again. He slowly moved me until he could cradle me in his arms and bring me in to his chest. "Leave me. I beg you!" I tried to pull away, but his arms were tight with me in them.

"Olive, I will not leave you," he said softly as he cradled me in his arms. I felt his hand stroke my coarse hair.

"I've lost my powers. I've lost my powers." I sobbed.

"I'm so sorry, Olive. So very sorry." He attempted to pull my hair back to see my face.

That made me sob all the louder, as I clutched my face to prevent him from seeing, "Please, don't. Please! I cannot imagine how I look, but Victore's face...I know what it must be. Now. Forever."

Bart seemed undeterred, his hand still stroked my hair as he continued to cradle me. He spoke so gently, "I saw the ships swallowed by the sea. I saw the lightning bolt. You did it, Olive. You saved us all." He gently touched my left hand and attempted to pull it from my face.

I resisted. I knew he would be disgusted by me now, just as my father was when he first saw my mother.

"And I know that magic must have been very hard," he continued in his calm, soft voice, "very difficult. And I know what it must have cost you. You are very brave, Olive. Very brave, my dear Olive."

I finally let him move back half of my hair. I knew he could see part of my face – the new destruction. I looked up at him at last and feared what I would see in his eyes, but his face was nothing but tender.

"Olive. Olive." he cooed my name as his hand slowly touched my face. I wiped away my tears and finally looked him in the eye and was met with only acceptance. "How could you think this would matter to me? I see you, Olive. I see all of the magic in you."

He was staring into my eyes and I felt like he could truly see me. I collapsed into his chest as the relief washed over me. He continued to cradle me in his arms and hold me close. I had never felt so protected in my life, so safe, as in the arms of this highwayman.

"What will become of me, Bart? I've lost my powers. I've lost everything. The treaty…" I stifled another sob as I realized how much my future had changed. What future?

"I don't think there's need of a treaty anymore, not after you've destroyed all of our enemy," Bart tried to soothe me.

"Now, the Prince will never marry me. Not that I wanted to marry him. I mean, I didn't. But at least before, I had a choice." I knew I was talking like an idiot. I had never wanted to marry the Prince. The only man I would ever consider marrying was holding me in his arms.

Bart stroked my hair and smiled, "Then I will tell the King of your infinite beauty."

That made me choke with its ridiculousness and I even smiled, "Do not mock me." I gave him a slight shove, "He would think himself tricked when he actually laid his eyes upon me and would only be all the more cruel."

Bart looked me in the eye, "No, I know him well. I will tell the King of your courage and of your beauty, dear Olive."

The way he looked at me then was a revelation – he looked serious! "I beg you, Bart. Do not humiliate me! I shall never marry now. I know that, I chose that." I began to gather some of my strength back. "The Prince can marry my sister and be well pleased with her beauty, just as my father planned." How could it be that I had only left my home yesterday morning to set out on my journey? So much had changed.

"Perhaps that might be good for me?" He stared into my eyes, "That you might then be available?" he stated sweetly. He released me from his arms, and moved to his knees and held my hands in his. I couldn't help but smile my reply.

"Olive?" I heard a familiar voice call out my name. I looked down the beach to the north, thousands of soldiers were galloping down the shoreline and in the lead was my father. "OLIVE!" he called again.

I jumped up and raised my hand in acknowledgment, then looked back to Bart. I had only seen him look nervous on one other occasion, and he had the same look about him now.

"Speak of the devil, there he is," he almost whispered. He looked into my eyes, "He must not see me for he knows I have worked for King Ivan and may think me a mercenary only fit for the edge of his blade." He quickly stood, and clasped my hand momentarily, "Forgive me, but I must go, dear Olive."

I noticed he was keeping his back to my father as he did so. He then jumped onto his horse and road off in the opposite direction without further delay. I watched him go, disappointed, "So much for not leaving me." I mumbled to no one in particular. I fluffed my hair obscuring my face in anticipation of my father's arrival, this would not be pretty.

I was so angry at my father. This had all been his fault. But in a way, I suppose, if he hadn't put the wheels in motion, we would never have found out about the Druzazzi and at this moment, our country would be in the process of being slaughtered at their hand and Victore's. My father's stupidity had allowed us to stop it all. I'd never give him the satisfaction of knowing that.

I heard his horse riding up the bluff. I splayed my hair around my face to cover it. I could still make him out, but more importantly, he couldn't make me out. Not yet, anyway.

He was decked out in his finest armor, his yellow cape cascading about him as he brought his horse to a halt in front of me, "Daughter! What have you done?" he demanded.

I kept my head down as I answered him, trying to keep the anger from my voice, "I've sunk the entire fleet of the Druzazzi, Father."

He leapt off of his horse, and stalked over to Victore's dead body and gave it a sharp kick, "Traitor!" he hissed at him. Then he moved over to where I sat, and smugly looked down at me, "Imagine my surprise to learn of this plot from an owl. You must tell me how this happened."

"I was kidnapped by a highwayman on my way to you." I responded, trying to keep from screaming at him.

"A highwayman? But why were *you* coming?"

He couldn't keep the sneer from his voice. Why should I expect anything different? "I wanted to rescue you, Father."

He smirked at me, "You never even made it to the castle," then let out a conceited snicker. "Besides, as you well know, that message was meant for Roseline and she wasn't expected for a fortnight."

"That's not what the message said." I looked up at him at last and got the reaction I expected. He looked like he was going to vomit.

He quickly glanced around to ensure no one else had seen me, that there were no witnesses to his shame. "My God, Olive. What has happened to you?!" He unclasped his cape and threw it at me. "Hide yourself. I must get you out of here."

I took the cape and wrapped myself in it because I knew it would be cold tonight. I turned and looked at my father, "I'm not coming with you."

"What do you mean — *you're not coming with me*!? I am your Father! I am the KING! You will do what I say!" He roared at me.

"Or what, Father? You'll cut off my crux? Your beloved Victore already took care of that for you!" I waved my hand in the air at him. "I am sick to death of your constant scorn and derision! Today, I saved our country — AGAIN!" I screamed at him. "You and every other person in this land have *me* to thank for your lives!" I turned my back on him and marched off in the direction of the forest.

"Olive!" he decreed. "You will obey me."

"Father," I turned and glared at him, "I will not obey you until you learn to see me as I am, past this external shell!" I turned my eyes to Victore's dead body, "It is beyond me how you could treasure a fool like him over your own flesh and blood! He wanted to kill you and I have saved you — twice! Yet still, you do not love me!" I shrieked at him, then turned and ran into the forest.

15

Heart Break

As I stomped away into the forest, my father's screaming voice began to fade. How dare he chastise me! I wiped the tears from my eyes – how could I have any left? But his face, the scorn he looked at me with...I was just glad I hadn't let him see how badly he had hurt me. Better to cry these tears in private then let him think I was weak. *I was not weak! I was Olive and I had saved my people!*

I tried to take great comfort in that thought. How my grandmother had helped me, the rest of my dead sisters. It was horribly ironic that minutes after I had finally understood how my powers worked, they were taken from me. I let out a gasp of sorrow and tried not to think about it for a moment. For half a second. But how could I not? How could I not think of how my life was now completely ruined? How would I even be able to tell my friends what had happened?

I trudged up the hillside behind the bluff through the forest and listened for them. This is where I had told them to wait for me. And then I heard a soft growl.

There next to the tree ahead was Bear. I ran the last steps to him and embraced him. He was growling softly in my ear. They were words of comfort I'm sure, but I couldn't understand them. I looked into his beautiful brown eyes, "I can no longer understand you, dear friend."

His ears perked up in surprise as I knew he could no longer understand my words either. A look of anger filled his face and his growl was harsh.

I held out my hand, showing him the black scar, "Victore." I started to act it out for him, but being such a poor actor, I wasn't sure he understood.

Bear let out such a roar of pain, it made me jump. He did understand. I even acted out how Bart had shot him and Victore was dead and when he growled, it almost sounded like, "good."

When I looked back into his eyes, I knew the pain was not directed at me, but for the loss of the Last of the Winnowwood for the Bestiallas. Our days were now over, unless I had a daughter. How I would pray that someday I would have a daughter.

I ran my hand along his face then hugged him hard in comfort for us both. When I pulled away, I pointed at myself, "One day, Bear, I will have a daughter." And I placed my arms together like I was rocking a child.

Though his eyes were filled with sadness, his eyes also showed he knew that there was still hope. He growled softly and nodded his head. Then I followed him as he led me back to where the Bestiallas waited for me.

That night, wrapped in my father's cape surrounded by my animals, I stared up at the stars. My friends had all been heart-broken when Bear explained what had happened, yet, they still loved me. They would not abandon me though if they had wanted, they could rip me to shreds for no magic protected me now. Their love was unconditional, as mine was for them.

I had ridden one of the horses back to the glen. I had to start a fire with a flint rock, which took a while since I was out of practice. There had been supplies for me in the little shed, some dried fruit, and water from the lake of course. I avoided looking at myself in the reflection of the lake, plenty of time to find a way to deal with that reality later.

Later when I laid down, wrapped in my Father's warm cape, I studied the stars and I reflected on all that had happened: I had saved our lands and we were safe. I tried to think of that thought when my spirit was falling into utter darkness. Last night, I thought we were doomed, yet tonight, we still lived. We were still here and they were all dead. I don't like to think of myself as heartless, but it cheered me that the Druzazzi now slept at the bottom of the sea and would not be able to harm us again.

Next to me lay Side Stripe with the Grey Mouse and Brown Mouse nestled next to him. It would appear my little mouse friend from Bart's cave had found her true love. That made me smile, as I watched them nuzzle each other.

As I drifted off to sleep, my mind wanted to focus on how it felt when I was in Bart's arms when he had hugged me, the look in his eyes when he had seen my destroyed face, and his almost last words when he seemed to imply that he wanted to marry me. Could that truly be the case? I clung to that hope as I drifted into a deep sleep. Perhaps, I would have a daughter. I would name her Aurelia — my golden child.

The next morning when I woke, I decided to face my fears and try to find Bart. I needed to know if he really did have feelings for me. I no longer cared in the slightest that he was a highwayman, which made me smile to myself.

I thought back to that first time we had met when I had continually derided him for being a thief and completely beneath me. Yet, in the few days since that time, he had proven himself to be the best man that I had ever met.

Highwayman or not, I wanted to be with him. If only he would have me.

I walked over to the lake to fetch some water and was feeling brave for some foolish reason. I took a deep breath and decided to face my fear, so I looked in. The water was still and reflected all with the perfection of a mirror. I gasped in shock, all of my breath left me as I gazed at my image, my knees grew weak beneath me.

Bear came up next to me and I braced myself against him. He growled with pleasure as I looked at myself, because I could see myself as he saw me — I was the most beautiful creature I had ever beheld. I was more than stunning, more than breath-taking. I stood there staring at this magical creature staring back at me and I smiled and she smiled back at me.

I let out a hard laugh, "Oh, beautiful Olive trapped in this hideous shell." My hand went to my face to ensure what my reality was and traced over the multitude of warts, the lumps and the bumps. I stared back down at the Venus in the water as she ran her hand over her perfect, lustrous skin. Her hair shone like polished copper hanging in ringlets to her waist. Only in her eyes did I see anything of myself. Her eyes filled with tears as she looked at me with a strange smile on her lips.

It was odd to stare at this girl who had nothing in common with me except the green eyes. It certainly didn't feel like I was looking at myself, but a person I had never met before. I thought about how my life would be if I looked like the girl in the water. In all truth, I wasn't sure if I would like it. I'd watched as men made fools of themselves in front of my mother my entire life and never envied her. How could one ever know if someone truly loved them or just loved what their eyes fell in love with? At least I would always know that Bart loved me for me, if he did love me, and that made me happy. I smiled and the girl in the water smiled back so beautifully.

"I bet you wouldn't have been able to save your country," I challenged her. She looked back at me searching for an answer. "You'd be a coward like my sister!" I glared back at her and met her equally stern glare. I kept staring at this stranger and couldn't unlock any of her secrets.

"So, this is how it feels to be beautiful," I said softly to Bear knowing he couldn't understand my words. But when I looked at him, I swear he did. His face was somber, then he bowed before me as if I did still retain my powers.

I fell to my knees and hugged him. I tried not to cry for my loss, for what would never be. At least all the warts and marks on my face were for something – for the people and animals I loved. I couldn't have regrets, not now.

As I neared Bart's hide-out, my heart began to pound frantically in my chest. I was so nervous to face him again. During my ride, I had convinced myself that it was only the heat of the battle that had made Bart say those words to me.

That once reality set in, he would run screaming from me, like every other man I had ever met.

I rode with my father's cape around me with the hood pulled up far over my face so that it would be hidden in shadows from anyone who looked at me. Hopefully, my father's crest would ensure my safety as well as assistance from other travelers I came across.

I looked up and saw a small flock of birds flying high overhead. I knew Bear had sent them to keep an eye on me and they would surely report back to him if I needed any assistance. There was also a pack of wolves only about a hundred yards behind me as well, if my ears were accurate. I could hear their soft growls as they spoke to each other.

And lastly, Side Stripe with the two mice on his head followed right behind me. He seemed determined to act as my personal protector. I was most assuredly protected, but they would not be able to protect my heart if Bart decided to break it. My horse started down the river bank to the entrance to Bart's cave and my pulse raced in anticipation of seeing him again.

Two soldiers were standing guard outside when we approached. "What is your business here?" one shouted to me.

"I seek Black Bart. I am a friend of his," I stated firmly.

The guard moved closer to my horse, trying to get a look at me, "Your name?"

"I am Princess Olive."

Both of the men snapped to attention, then saluted me with a fierceness I was not used to, "My Princess!" One turned and ran into the cave.

The other who remained seemed bashful now. "May I take this opportunity to uh, thank you, M'lady," he bowed formally. "I was with you on the beach," he paused again, "You saved us all, my Princess."

I nodded my head low in return, "I thank you for your courage on the beach as well. For holding them off until I was able to help."

"Thank you, M'lady," he said with utter solemnity.

At that moment, Geraldo appeared from out of the cave entrance, "My Princess, it is good to see you," he gave me a short bow.

"It is good to see you as well, Geraldo. I was hoping to speak with Bart."

"I'm sorry, My Princess. He left this morning for Alganoun Castle. He said he had an urgent matter to discuss with King Ivan."

That almost made me gasp with horror, he'd better not discuss me with King Ivan! That would be incredibly humiliating.

Geraldo moved closer to my horse and spoke in a quiet voice, "Perhaps you are unaware, Princess, but King Ivan is hosting a ball this evening in celebration of the victory. I am told that Bart expected you to be there as King Ivan is holding it in your family's honor."

"I was not aware of that, sir." The idea of a ball and seeing King Ivan made my heart beat all the faster. Certainly, Bart wouldn't embarrass me in front of the entire court.

Geraldo must have noticed my silence and continued on with his explanation, "I believe your father is announcing your sister's betrothal to the Prince this evening."

"Of course," I let out a breath of relief as I realized Bart's plan. He would be there for me as he discussed. My sister could have the Prince and I would have my happiness at last – or so I prayed. "I will go there directly."

"Please, let me send an escort with you, Princess," Geraldo offered.

"There is no need. I am well protected, trust me," I assured him.

I turned and began my journey to Alganoun, knowing all of my hopes for any happiness for my future laid there.

16

Alganoun

It was close to dusk when I spied the turrets of Alganoun Castle high on the hill in front of me. I kept one hand on Side Stripe as I rode onwards. I had stopped and picked him up shortly after leaving Bart's hide-out, as I needed to make good time and didn't like the thought of the little Fox running the entire way behind me. He quickly became quite adept at keeping his seat in front of my saddle, clinging to the horse's mane as the little mice clung to his ears.

As I approached the gate, I stopped to take it all in, after all, I had only seen it from the sky before. Alganoun: it was a magnificent work of architectural wonder. While my own castle was stunning in its own right, this castle intimidated you with its sheer immensity, its countless turrets and huge battlements surrounded by a wide moat with hundreds of blue banners flapping in the evening breeze.

Would Bart be waiting for me here? After Father announced my sister's betrothal, would he rescue me from my futureless life? The only future I now wanted was with him. I would be very content living in a cave with Bart. That put a smile on my lips, then I laughed to myself.

Side Stripe and the mice looked up at me curiously. "I'm looking forward to living in a cave...I must love him." I gave Side Stripe a gentle pat and let out another chuckle.

I advanced to the drawbridge at the main gate and was met by the Captain of the Guard, a heavy-set man who looked a bit familiar. He stopped next to my horse, "Identify yourself!"

"It is I, Princess Olive. I have been invited to attend your celebration," I replied.

A look of awe came on his face and he immediately bowed, "My Princess, please, welcome to Alganoun!" He turned to the other guards, "Make way for Princess Olive!"

The rest of the guard snapped to attention, "My Princess!" they shouted as I rode across the drawbridge. A few of them looked familiar, and I wondered if they too had been on the beach with me. As I rode through the gates, I pushed my hood back, not all the way, I wasn't that brave, but far enough where they could partially see the shadow of my face because I wanted to look at theirs. To the last man, their faces were filled with respect and admiration. I sat up straighter in my saddle, I nodded to them as I passed and each saluted in turn. It would seem I was with friends at Alganoun.

My mother inspected my new black scar, moving my hand back and forth as if that would change anything. We were in the suite of rooms my family had been given for our stay. The rooms were luxurious and Roseline was busying herself inspecting all of the beautiful items which filled the rooms. I think it was giving her some sense of consolation to be gaining such riches even if she didn't love the Prince. She ran her hand down a perfectly carved, life-sized sculpture of a beautiful young woman in pink marble, then moved on to examine a golden bowl set with emeralds and sapphires the size of acorns that sat on an elegant armoire.

Fresh flowers filled the rooms and a buffet of delectable food had been set out for our enjoyment. My room had a beautiful arrangement of lilies in it that reminded me of the ones that had been in my room at Bart's hide-out. It sent a thrill down my spine to know that somewhere in this palace was Bart.

I ran my hand along the silk cloth of the divan and enjoyed the feel of the material against my fingers and my thoughts of him. I was still nervous, still worried that he might have changed his mind, but I longed to see him.

"Tell me how this happened," Mother demanded, her face filled with sadness for me.

"Victore took the Blade of the Winnowwood from me, then he cut off my finger with his own dagger, so I am lost." I looked over to my sister, "*Your* beautiful, darling Victore."

I will say Roseline looked far paler then when I had seen her last. She glared at me, "Don't speak to me of that traitor!"

Perhaps it wasn't fair, but I couldn't help but bait her a bit, "Do you mean to tell me you do not mourn his death? Really Sister, is your heart that hard?"

But she would have none of it as she attacked back, "Oh shut up, Olive! You should have listened to me long ago and cut off that ugly stump, then you wouldn't be sitting here in that repulsive shell!" She almost looked smug as she chastised me, "I'm sure you regret not listening to me now?"

"I regret nothing!" I roared back at her, "I did my duty! I saved this country!"

Roseline's voice spit with venom, "And now you shall have to live with the consequences! Do you think you will be lauded? You will be ostracized! You're so hideous —"

Mother stepped in, "That is quite enough! I am incredibly proud of Olive as we all should be. She paid this price to save us from those horrific barbarians!" Mama took me in her arms and held me.

I stared at my sister, shocked at her hateful words, then she began to cry and flung herself next to me, "Mother's right. I'm so sorry, Olive. It's just I loved Victore so much and to find out he was this wicked pretender...I feel like such a fool!" she broke into loud sobs, crying on my shoulder.

My mother's gentle eyes watched me then looked at my sister and shook her head, "Stop taking your sadness out on your poor sister. She has suffered far more than you from Victore's actions," she scolded Roseline.

I looked over to Side Stripe, who was lying in front of the hearth enjoying the warmth of the fire with the mice. With all the yelling, he was nervous for me — his tail twitching restlessly as he watched.

Then the door was flung open and Father appeared. He held an open scroll in his hand, "Good news! All of the details are set for our families to be united in marriage." He grasped Roseline's hand and pulled her to her feet, "He will announce it tonight!"

His face was filled with joy as he let out a laugh of utter glee, "This is exactly what I wanted! Roseline shall be the Queen of all of Alganoun and Rosemount. She shall unite a nation. Excellent!" He grabbed her by the waist and swung her around as she giggled. He finally put her down and was a bit out of breath, red-faced, but still grinned.

Roseline beamed with delight under the warm approval of my father's eyes. I know I shouldn't have taken the bait, but it irritated me. "I thought you would never consider marrying such a — what was it? An ugly frog of a man?"

My sister looked at me and found her own spine again, "A girl must do her duty. Haven't you taught me that, Sister?"

"Then true love is no more an obstacle?" I asked sweetly.

Roseline paused, but she knew what she was made of, "I will love his money and power very truly indeed." She smiled at me, but a look of defeat was in her eyes. "I must prepare myself. I do want to look well for the Courtiers, Lord Rupert is quite handsome." She lifted her head and sauntered out of the room.

The look in her eyes finally silenced any retort from me. I was being cruel and that was not like me. Roseline would marry someone she did not love. All of the fantasies that she had lived for, obsessed over, and she would not have any of them. Then I thought of Bart and knew I would be happy. I was the lucky one.

Father stood before my mother and me, obviously uncomfortable to be in my presence. "Yes, well. We'd all better prepare." He glared down at me, clearly still angry, "And you will wear a veil, Olive. A good thick one." He looked at my mother, "See to it."

My mother nodded, then he quickly stalked out of the room. She looked back at me and ran her hand gently along my damaged face. "Tell me of this highwayman who kidnapped you. He sounds like the worst sort of man."

For a moment, I didn't say anything. I was almost afraid to say how I felt out loud, almost as if that would make it too real. I chose real. "No, he is the kindest, bravest, truest man I have ever known. He's the only man who has looked past my face and into my heart." I paused as I thought of Bart, "He is a true gentleman."

My mother's green eyes examined me, "Strange words from you."

"Yes, I know. But he..." I could feel myself smile, "...he's the one that made me understand how my powers work."

"How could he know that?" she asked with a surprised look on her face, after all, she had never known how to use her powers either.

I took her hands in mine. "It was simple actually. It's love. That's why it was always so easy for me to heal my animals, because I loved them so much. And it was love that gave me the power to make those winds that destroyed their fleet. I could finally feel my power and it was so amazing, Mama. I knew that I could save our people and I was no longer afraid. And in the midst of it, Grandmother came and helped me!"

My mother's face smiled with joy, "Mother was there?"

"Yes. Her spirit was beside me as we called the winds, then our other dead sisters joined us as well. It was amazing. Unbelievable, really. And then minutes after finding out the secret of my powers, I lost them." I let out a long sigh of sadness, "I am lost."

I slumped against my mother's shoulder and she held me close in her arms. "My brave, beautiful girl," she whispered to me as she stroked my coarse hair. "But how did this highwayman know the secret to your powers?"

"He told me how he had mastered his own fears in battle. How he would think of all of the people he loved and it would clear his mind and that I should try it. He was right. Once I was no longer fearful, I could feel the power in me."

"He does sound like an unusual man," she looked closely at me. "Do you love him, Olive?"

I had given too much away. I didn't want to reveal myself before I knew if it was real, but as I looked my mother in the eyes, I had to tell the truth, "Yes. I love him with all my heart."

Mother's eyes filled with concern, she was silent for a few moments before she spoke. "Probably best not to let your father know for now."

I couldn't help but smile, "Yes, Mama. I couldn't agree more."

17

The Prince

I stood in front of the mirror in my room taking myself in. I rarely wore my Princess crown as I thought it looked rather silly sitting in my wild haystack of hair, but tonight demanded that formality. My mother had given me a beautiful dress of gold silk for me to wear to the ball, but it didn't help my face. At this moment, I surely didn't feel like the lucky one. Instead, I was filled with anxiety.

I had finally counted all of the warts: one hundred and twenty-two, accompanied by three lumps of varying sizes, a large bump and two boils. I could feel the tears begin to start and I blinked them away. Fine to be nervous, but I promised myself that I would not cry, not because of this.

I wondered if in the history of the world there had ever been a Princess as ugly as me? I doubted it. But was there ever a Princess in the history of the world who saved their kingdom twice from annihilation by the time they were eighteen, and I doubted that as well. I gave myself a brave smile then attached the veil to my crown and appraised myself — well, it was a beautiful dress.

There was a knock at the door, then my mother entered. She, of course, looked her usual stunning self, "Are you ready?"

I wished I could avoid the formalities and join them later after all of the introductions, but I knew I had to go. I took a deep breath, then turned to follow her. I felt a paw on my dress and looked down — Side Stripe was pulling on the hem of my dress. "So, you still think I need protection?" I smiled down at him.

He pawed at my dress again, the little mice still upon his head. I lifted my skirt and he ran under it. At least I would have friends accompanying me into this trial. I just prayed that Bart had not spoken to King Ivan.

The ball was being held outside under the full moon in the courtyard. As we turned the corner at the top of the stairs, I stopped to take it all in. Beautiful decorations of both blue and yellow banners filled the courtyard as well as rippled in the breeze from the turrets above. Multitudes of torches lit the night sky and the air was filled with lovely music.

Eight giant oak trees towered on the edges of the immense courtyard. I noticed something moving in one of the largest trees and my mouth fell open. High up in its branches was Bear! How had he managed to sneak into the castle?

He was well-hidden and must have only moved to let me see him. I gave him a small waved. The tree shook lightly in response. Dear Bear, my dedicated servant and counselor; at least he liked Bart as well. I wasn't looking forward to telling my father I was running away with a highwayman, but I had made my decision. I loved him. He was a gift I never thought possible for a girl like me. How many men would ever look past my superficial hideous shell and see me? Only Bart. I believed in him, and that made me believe the words he had spoken to me were true. I knew it in my heart, he was true and I would not let my own insecurities talk be out of that or doubt him.

My mind raced with the possibilities. If I could just survive the initial formalities, Bart would find me later and we could escape together. I wondered if he would dare show himself, or perhaps he might be in a disguise as he seemed so fearful of Father seeing him. All I knew was my new life with him would start tonight and that made me happier than I could ever have imagined. I chuckled to myself as I knew I would not have to learn the recipe for that potion to drug unsuspecting men in the forest.

My sister glanced back at me when she heard my laughter, "Are you alright, Sister?"

"I am perfect, do not worry yourself."

She nodded at me, then turned back around to follow Mother and Father. Roseline was wearing a gown of yellow and blue as a symbol of the union she was about to enter in to. Of course, she looked stunning, but I could still see a sadness in her eyes that touched me. I was the fortunate one, at least I would have the love of my life.

I looked past the stairs into the courtyard — what a spectacle! It was already crowded with expensively dressed courtiers. Every Earl, Baron, Duke, and Lord with their Ladies in all of the lands must be present. An army of servants dashed about attending to their every need. Around the perimeter of the courtyard, well over a hundred soldiers in their finest armor stood at attention, each held a tall spear in their right hand.

At the end of the courtyard was a raised platform that held an ornate jewel-encrusted throne, which was occupied by King Ivan. *Oh, please, Bart, I pray you have not spoken to him about me.* This was a far larger crowd to be humiliated in front of than I ever could have imagined. My heart leapt in my chest at the thought of it.

I followed behind my parents and sister in front of me. When we reached the top of the stairs, the music stopped.

The shout of the Court Herald broke the silence, "Your Majesty, King Michael and Queen Opal of Rosemount and Princess Roseline and Princess Olive.

A hush fell over the crowd and all eyes turned to watch us. My parents began their descent of the stairs looking supremely regal. Then Roseline paraded after them, perfection in every way. I tried to keep my head up, yet not to trip down the stairs, as the veil did impair my vision. I supposed Father wouldn't care if I fell down these stairs and broke my neck as long as my veil remained over my face. But I would not fall, not tonight. I made it to the bottom unscathed and continued to follow my sister.

When we had made it to the platform that held King Ivan, he stood to greet us and bows and curtsies were exchanged between us.

Father, looking like he would nearly bust with pride, stepped forward, "King Ivan, may I present my daughter: Princess Roseline."

Father moved back to allow Roseline to step forward. My sister curtsied again, then smiled up at him with the face of an angel.

King Ivan stepped down from his platform then extended his hand to take Roseline's and gave her a kind smile, "You are indeed lovely, my dear."

"Thank you, your majesty," Roseline purred her reply as she stood.

King Ivan looked back at my father, his eyes twinkled like he had a secret, "But I have been told by a most trusted source, that your beauty pales in comparison to that of your sister's."

"Olive!" Roseline shrieked in shock, the purr had left her.

Oh no, oh no! Bart has ruined everything! My mind was reeling that he had done what he had said he would do. I truly had thought he was kidding me. *How could he do this to me?* In mere seconds, I would be humiliated in front of everyone! *How could he torture me like this?* He must have the cruelest streak in him that I had not recognized. *I was such a fool! Perhaps he didn't care for me at all!* The little voice in my head was snickering away, "How could any man love you, didn't you look in the mirror before you left?"

I glanced over at Father and his face was even redder than that time when I was eleven and had appeared that fateful evening in the Grand Hall. He truly looked like he would explode, though he tried to keep his voice calm, "There is someone who plays a trick on you, sir. Roseline is my beauty."

As King Ivan made a step toward me, Father, horrified by the implication, attempted to block his way. At that moment, I was hoping that Father might tackle him, and then I could try to make an escape. But it was not to be.

King Ivan glared at him and Father was forced to step back, the vein on his temple throbbed wildly.

The King of Alganoun now stood in front of me. I curtsied as gracefully as I was able, "My father is quite correct. I'm afraid a dear friend has told you a lie, your Majesty."

He obviously couldn't see my face with the thick veil protecting it, but somehow I felt like he already knew me as he looked at me with such a peaceful countenance. "Are you not Princess Olive, the Last of the Winnowwood, who personally defeated the Druzazzi? Do I not have you to thank for saving our country?" He took my hand and I rose.

"But that is where it ends, your Majesty. I am far from beautiful, sir, in fact, quite the opposite." My heart was thumping wildly in my chest and I tried to calm it, to remember who I was for I knew what was coming.

He smiled at me, "You are the brave, courageous Olive of whom I have been told." He stepped forward and lifted his hand toward my veil.

I was ready. I knew who I was and I would *not* cry. I would not embarrass myself in front of all of these people no matter what my father thought. *I was Olive, Last of the Winnowwood, and I would not be afraid!*

He removed my veil.

I stared at him, prepared for a harsh reaction, but found none in King Ivan's eyes. Out of the corner of my eye, I could see my father's face filled with his agonizing shame. Prepared for the crowd's reaction, his head fell.

And he was right because I began to hear the gasps from the crowd, the loud whispers that filled the air and the long hisses.

"Hideous." "What a monster!" Finally, a clear voice from the back of the crowd said it all: "She is an ugly Princess!"

I will not bend to this. I will not be shamed! I held my head higher.

For a couple of seconds, there was complete silence, then from the side, I heard the first shout, "My Princess!" and a spear struck the cobblestone of the courtyard in a loud clank.

Then another shouted out, "My Princess!" and struck his spear to the ground.

In seconds, all of the guards in unison began to shout, "My Princess!" as their spears hit together in a rhythmic fury unto the ground.

All of the Courtiers were now silent as the cries of the guards filled the night, "MY PRINCESS! MY PRINCESS! MY PRINCESS!" and the sound of their spears thumping onto the stone echoed in the air. For well over a minute, King Ivan allowed the guards' tribute to me to fill the air.

I was overwhelmed by it. By their loyalty. By their love. Tears of joy sprang to my eyes as I let their song of respect wash over me. I was so thankful to them at this moment. I looked over to Father whose face was filled with amazement and confusion for he could not understand why they would cheer me.

Finally, King Ivan held up his hand and the soldiers immediately stopped their cries.

I stood tall, my pride restored, "As you can see, Majesty, you have been lied to, as you are not blind."

"Indeed, my sight is clear and I know you are the woman my son will love," he said with satisfaction.

"Then I hope he is the one who is blind, sir." I smiled ironically at King Ivan.

But from the side, I heard a familiar voice, "I am not blind, Olive."

And there he was — Bart, but no longer a highwayman — clean shaven, in royal garments with a crown on his head! My mouth dropped open in amazement. Bart now stood in front of me next to King Ivan.

King Ivan grinned at me, "Princess Olive, may I present my son: Prince Bartholomew."

I was so confused, I could barely speak, "Bart?"

Bart smiled at me, "Father, may I present the most beautiful woman of my acquaintance, for my heart is lost to her and I must make her my wife."

I was still stunned, but managed to blurt out, "But I thought you a highwayman?!"

Bart smiled his wonderful smile at me that was filled with amusement at my shock, "That was just a ruse for espionage for my father's sake during the war. Though I dare say, a rather profitable one."

"But, I don't understand. If you are the Prince, why did you kidnap me?"

"I thought a beautiful Princess was to marry me in a fortnight as part of a peace treaty. But I am an ugly man, and knew she would never love me looking as I do." He took my hands into his, "I hoped if I kidnapped her, then in the time we spent together, before we formally met, as it were, that she would learn to love me as I am. I hope it worked."

He looked at me with such acceptance, admiration and love that I was flooded with emotion, "Indeed it did, sir." *He had never meant to embarrass me; he had only spoken the truth to me.* I stared at him with the same adoration I had seen on Roseline's face when she had looked at Victore. But it was such a different face that stared back at him, yet, he loved me. How could he be so true?

Bart took his hand and touched my scarred face, oh, so gently, then stared into my eyes and I swear he could see me as I was, "And I am overwhelmed with your beauty, my dear Olive. I love you so."

A lightning bolt flashed across the sky, then white, glittering dust that almost looked like snow began to fall from the sky.

Bart and I were both staring, watching the glittering clusters dance in the air. "What is this? More magic of yours?" he asked.

"I have no idea." but suddenly I felt a warm glow in my left hand. I held it up in front of us and we watched as out of the black scar a glowing white spot appeared, then a new crux grew back on my left hand in seconds. I was restored!

"Olive, it's back! Oh, if only you had the Blade of the Winnowwood!" Roseline shrilly cried out.

Bart casually reached into his pocket, then hung something around my neck — the Blade of the Winnowwood. That's what he had removed from Victore. "She does possess the blade," he calmly stated.

Roseline's face was filled with hope for me, "Thank the Gods! Cut it off now while you have the chance!" she earnestly decreed.

My father's voice joined in as well, "Cut it now, Olive," he ordered me.

"No!" Bart's voice echoed mine at exactly the same moment I spoke. I looked at him and smiled like I was going to burst. Indeed, this man did love me for me! I was overcome with emotion.

Bart just continued to smile at me, clasping my hands tightly in his. He turned to Roseline, "Give away such a gift for beauty? She's not stupid." He looked back at me, "That's only in case we have foolish daughters."

"Pity our children," I laughed with him.

"Never! What they may lack for in appearance will be made up for with courage and strength of character." He looked into my eyes with the sincerest of expressions, "Will you honor me by becoming my wife, Olive?"

There was no hesitation on my part, I was beyond any happiness I could have imagined, "Yes, my dear Bart. I would have been the wife of a highwayman."

"Then this is better," he glibly replied. He took me into his arms and kissed me.

As his lips touched mine, I was filled with warmth from my head to my toes. *So, this is what love feels like*, I thought. Amazing. Then it got hotter. And hotter. There was something wrong. My body was stiffening. I could still hear the rattling of the soldiers' spears as they cheered, but I was being paralyzed and in seconds I couldn't move.

Bart stepped away from me and we both watched horrified as a greenish-golden skin began to cover me. I saw Side Stripe with the mice move out from under my dress as sparks flew from my hair. I watched as the golden shell moved up my arms and over my shoulders. The last thing I saw was Bart's horror-struck face. I was blind and couldn't move.

18

Revelation

It felt like I had been filled with hot liquid, but it wasn't that uncomfortable, more of a feeling of electricity flowing through me that possessed my body. Then I heard my grandmother's voice in my mind, "Do not be afraid. Do not be afraid, dear Olive." Other voices of my fallen sisters joined hers, all of them soothing me, comforting me to not be afraid. "You are legend," Grandmother whispered to me. "Legend," the hundreds of voices whispered to me. I was calm. I did not let the loss of my senses overwhelm me.

The heat that filled my body seemed to emanate from my newly formed crux. My left arm was the conduit to the rest of my body, which tingled to each nerve fiber, as the warmth passed through my body electrifying me with its power. Light danced against my eyelids, flashes of green and gold. It was not painful, it felt more that I was being filled with an awesome power that filled every cell of my being. But still I could not move. And the lullaby of my grandmother, my sisters, continued the entire time as they whispered, "You are legend."

Before my blind eyes, green dreamlike images of every Winnowwood who had ever lived and died passed before me. Each only whispered the same words, "You are legend." Then they reached out with their left hand and grasped my left hand for a brief moment. Their crux touched my crux and I felt some of their power pass into me. It was overwhelming. They were giving me all of their secrets to my powers! Images from their minds passed into mine, just like when I healed animals. I could see their histories, their magic, their triumphs. And it wasn't like I was going to have to remember everything on my own – their memories were now part of my consciousness. I could no more forget their memories than I could my own.

I felt like I wasn't big enough to hold it all, that I might soon burst at the seams. My mind raced over the images it now contained: how to control the weather, powerful spells, taming dragons, enchanting sea monsters, killing witches and so much more.

Images flew past me and lodged into my brain. I wanted to stop and examine each one, but of course, there was not time. Hundreds of my Winnowwood sisters passed before me, filling me with their magic and memories.

One of the last Winnowwood touched my crux and an immense power flowed into me. I looked into her beautiful eyes and she smiled at me knowingly — it was Ursula! She held my hand for a few seconds longer than the others and in those precious seconds, I saw her secrets and her heart and I was overwhelmed. Her story was beyond belief and my connection to her was now permanent. It made me feel invincible, but she gave me a look of caution, "Careful. All will be jealous of your power. Tell no one what we have shown you." With that warning, she left me.

Finally, the last Winnowwood came to me: my grandmother. She touched my hand, but instead of magic or spells, I was filled with the love she felt for Greatpapa. I gasped with raw emotion. She put her right hand against my cheek, "There is nothing as powerful as love. There is nothing that will bring you more joy than love. Bless you, my dear child, that you will be as happy as I was." She smiled, then was gone and my world turned to black.

I don't know how much time had passed, but I thought I heard someone whisper my name. It was Bart. Then, what sounded like the crackling of a bolt of lightning struck, and my shell crumbled away in a bright, shimmering green-golden light and I was myself.

Bart stared at me with a confused expression. I looked down and could see the copper ringlets falling to my waist. I knew what had happened — I had fulfilled the legend because of this man's love. I remembered the vision of the goddess in the water and realized that was now me.

It may seem insane, but at that moment, there was a big part of me that was disappointed. *The man I loved, loved me the way I was — warts and all.* I didn't know who this girl with the copper ringlets was, I had never cared about her. In fact, I was far less happy now than I was when Bart had asked me to marry him because he loved *me*, the real me, not the goddess.

I looked over to my father and his face was filled with a broad grin of adulation. Great. I really didn't want his adoration. I looked over to my sister, she looked saddened about being outshone, but then gave me a brave little smile. My mother's face was filled with joy as she cried out, "The legend has been fulfilled!"

Bart continued to stare at me in astonishment, "Olive, you have become the woman in the water."

I heard a cry from the crowd and I turned to face them, they all bowed and curtsied in submission to my beauty. That didn't impress me either. I knew what they really thought of me. But the loudest shouts were coming from a few standing on the aisle staring at the creature heading towards me. It was Bear.

I turned to Bart, who only smiled, "I thought you would want your best friend here."

"Thank you."

The Courtiers pulled back in fear, but none of the soldiers moved for they recognized him from the battle and knew he would do me no harm. "Bear!" I called out as he joined me and I hugged him.

"I knew you would fulfill the legend, dear Olive. All is as I foretold you: One day, a Prince will see your heart and will love you for who you are. His eyes will be clear and his heart as true as yours."

"I remember when you spoke those words and I thought you a fool," I whispered in his ear, "Thank you for always believing for me, even when I didn't."

"You believed," Bear emphatically declared. "If you had not, none of this could have happened.

"Actually, I was just hoping that this hadn't happened." I glanced around at all of the odd stares, but instead of stares of revulsion that I had grown used to, these new looks of adoration made me feel even more uncomfortable. "I never desired beauty, only to retain my powers and to speak with my friends."

"And that is why you are legend, Princess. All will be as I said — you will be blessed in all ways," he earnestly replied. "You must trust your fate."

I looked into his big, brown eyes and knew he understood my fears and misgivings over what my future would now hold. I knew he was right. All the blessings of my Winnowwood sisters had to be right. I kissed his nose then stood and turned to Bart.

I almost felt shy as I approached him, now that I was imprisoned in this body, which seemed so foreign to me. I finally dared to look him in the eye.

He stared back at me, then gave me a half of smile, "You're so beautiful, Olive, you'll never marry an ugly man like me." Then he smiled his wonderful smile, "I'll have to kidnap you for you to see my true self," and the look in his eyes showed he still saw just me, the real me, and I knew everything would be as it should.

As I stared at this amazing man, my heart melted, "My dear Bart. There is no need to kidnap me, for I am yours forever."

Side Stripe sat next to Bear, the mice still on his head, "Princess Olive! Princess Olive!" he cried out.

"Yes, my friend?"

"Can he finally see you as we do?" Side Stripe asked.

I looked back at Bart, "He saw me as I was long before this." With that, Bart took me into his arms and kissed me. This time the softness of his lips as they touched mine sent thrills of energy down to my very toes. This was truly how love felt, like I was home – in this man's arms, safe and loved. As his lips embraced mine, the little voice in my head whispered, "Lucky girl," and I knew it was right at last. This would be a love of legends and I could hardly wait to begin my new life.

Epilogue

When the ship appeared on the horizon, bells rang out. The soldiers who had been forced to remain behind to protect the city ran to the docks in anticipation of the news, aching to hear the details of the great victory that had surely occurred. Tonight, they would be regaled with the heroic stories of the conquerors, hear about the spoils that had been collected in the brilliant surprise attack upon their enemy and the death, all the details of the glorious deaths they had wrought on their enemy.

Yet, when the ship docked, there was no joviality to be found on board. Only its Captain spoke, "I need to see the King," he simply stated and left in a rush. The remaining crew only stared at them, under order of silence.

No matter the silence, the smell of defeat came off of each man. It could not be! The island people were soft. It was a surprise attack. It was impossible!

The Captain was on his knees before the King, his head bent in shame unable to meet the ice cold stare of his master. The master was an intimidating monster standing well over six-foot, with shoulders that seemed as wide as he was tall. His face reflected the battles he had survived, his eyes reflected the destruction he had wantonly released on his enemies. His lips were now pulled back into a mask of rage, "A witch! You tell me that a witch killed all of my men!"

The Captain whispered his reply, sure he was to die at any moment for his gross failure, "We found Ganius on the shore waiting for us. He had escaped during the first battle with the islanders. He said a witch flew to the top of the hills, then called the waves to do her bidding and sunk all of our ships. All the men drowned. All the ships destroyed."

"My son's ship?" he demanded, his face filled with fury.

"Was destroyed by an immense bolt of lightning. It was the last ship and had almost reached the shoreline."

"But we were told there were no witches that remained in the land!" he screamed, his voice resounding off the walls of the chamber. The King was then quiet for several seconds. He stared at the Captain, "And you only know this because you say your mast broke?"

"It delayed us for several hours, Sire."

The King's hand moved to the hilt of his sword.

The Captain bowed his head, prepared for death, "Ganius also said that your youngest son lives. He was taken prisoner by the Prince of Alganoun."

The King's hand paused, "You know the law."

EPILOGUE

The Captain bowed his head in submission, yes, he knew the law, knew his life was forfeit because of his defeat. And with a motion that was as experienced as the movement of the pendulum of a clock, the King's sword sliced the head cleanly off the Captain's shoulders.

The rusted iron door to the captive's cell was in the deepest bowels of the keep. She was not used to visitors and it sounded like a crowd was approaching. She knew they would come. Now. At this moment. She spent her days travelling in her mind, her powers still potent in many ways. She could feel her freedom approaching and she knew why.

She growled with delight when she thought of the irony of it all – her killing curse would now free her! It was a delicious premise given her current state of imprisonment. Her vanity had entrapped her in this prison over a hundred years ago, but now her curse would free her!

The key turned the lock in the door, noisily announcing their arrival. She kept her back to them, she knew who they were, what they wanted. There were four of them, but only he mattered. She was unable to curse them, they had prepared the cell too well with magic of their own, but she knew she now had the opportunity she had waited over a century for and she would use it to her ultimate advantage.

She could hear the King open his mouth to speak, and cut him off, "It was not a witch, King Viratrex." She could feel his confusion and slowly turned to him. "It was a Winnowwood. The Last of the Winnowwood, I believe."

He stared intently at her, "And how do you know this?"

She smiled at him, unnerving him further as he gazed upon her yellowed teeth while her black forked-tongue flicked like a snake's over them, "I will not reveal my secrets. Let us bargain, as you want your son and I want my freedom."

He continued to stare at her, momentarily unsure as to what to do, which must have tormented him mightily given his nature. Then she saw the small spark in his eye. He would do as she wanted, she could feel it, see it. "If you will release me, I will bind myself to you, in that I will not be able to betray you, and then I will kill this Winnowwood and rescue your son."

He stared into her cold black eyes and recognized a fellow traveler who adored evil with all of its might and power. He almost smiled, "Let it be so, Cassandra Dragon Slayer, and then you will have your freedom."

Acknowledgements

I am so lucky to have a family who believes in me and without their loving support, this book would not have been written. Thank you my dear ones: Peep, Bunny, Mosey, Booy & Freddy!

The beautiful cover of this book was created by Mikey Brooks. To see more of his work, please visit: insidemikeysworld.com.

Made in the USA
Middletown, DE
17 January 2017